Out of my Control

CJ Allison

Cover designed by CJ Allison
Cover Photo by R+M Photography, Melissa Deanching
Cover Model: Cody Smith
Editor: Debbie Barbosa Dumke from Two Naughty Book Babes Editing

CJ Allison
Visit my website at https://cjallisonauthor.wixsite.com/mysite

Dedication

It's all about love. It doesn't matter the sex or the reason. If you love someone, you love them. This is dedicated to all the people that have struggled with their sexuality and felt like they couldn't love who they wanted to because society told them they couldn't, and it was wrong. You are not wrong, society is. Fly your freak flag proud and love who you love, because when I see love, all kinds of love, it makes me smile.

Prologue

Patrick

I hear Logan yelling from his office.

"Patrick!"

"At your service, boss man," I say, trotting into his office.

"I'm moving to Tennessee," He says bluntly.

"Tell me something I didn't know," I respond, pretending to pick lint off of my pants and acting disinterested. Meanwhile, my heart skips a beat and starts to race.

Laughing, he says, "Okay, smart ass, elaborate."

"Logan. I know you better than you know yourself. You're a passionate man in everything you have ever done, but when it comes to this latest project, you have put in your soul. I've caught you numerous times when you are supposed to be working, simply staring and smiling at Presley Ann's picture on your desk. I've just been waiting for you to realize what you need to do."

I surprise myself on how calm I sound when I actually just want to scream.

"Well, I'm glad you know what I should be doing with my life. I guess I should have asked you a long time ago," He says, standing and looking out onto the city.

I walk over and stand next to him, bumping him with my shoulder I say, "Logan, I know you are doing the right thing. I want you to be happy. That's all I've ever wanted for you. It's your time. You deserve it."

He does. However, I'm so torn. I love Presley Ann and she is good for him. She is exactly what he needs. I just had held onto a fantasy that somehow; he would see me. I'm not stupid to think someone can suddenly turn gay. I just had this hope that our friendship would turn into something more. I know it's stupid. I just love him that much.

"Thanks," He says, draping his arm over my shoulder. "You know you are like family, right? Would you consider coming as well? I don't know how I will function without you being beside me on a daily basis."

His touch is too much. I want nothing more than to fold myself into him. Breathe him in and just be. I know that's not possible. Logan and I were never going to happen. A pipe dream that my foolish self kept imagining would come true. Even though, I knew it wouldn't.

I pull away and tuck my hands into my pockets. "I want to. I'm just not ready. Besides, you need this time to discover things with Presley Ann. You don't need little ol' me to be in the way."

I couldn't move there and be around all that happiness. I'm happy for him, I really am. I'm just bitter and it would be better if I'm not there.

"Patrick. You have never, ever been in the way. You make my life easier, and I honestly don't know how to function without you," He says, turning to me and mimicking my stance.

"You were fine in Tennessee without me. You survived Walmart without me. You'll have Presley Ann. You will be fine, and I'll still be here. It's not like I won't be your assistant. I'll just be remote. Once you get settled in, I'll come out every few months. Besides, there's a certain mountain man that I may or may not be interested in finding out more about. Who knows, I may be asking for a parcel of land as a bonus to build my own house," I say, giving him a sheepish smile.

I'm not lying. I just don't know if he's actually gay or even interested. However, he's been the only thing that has kept my sanity these last few weeks. The hope of something else.

"Oh really? Well then, it's a plan. You're amazing. You know that, right? You have helped me in every aspect of my life, and I'll always be grateful for you and I'm not letting you go. I know it's not your thing, but I also know that you felt the pull like I did. Those mountains and those people are simply amazing. Say you will at least consider it?" He almost begs.

"Logan, I can't tell you what tomorrow will bring. I'm a city boy. I love being able to walk out my door and walk two doors down to get a great cup of coffee. I love that I'm accepted here. There's always someone that will speak their mind about my lifestyle, but here it's a little more accepted. When talking to...him...it's so different there. I'm loud and I'm proud, and I don't think they are ready for me yet," I say with a catch in my voice.

He pulls me into a hug. "Dude. I can't imagine. I'm here for you and know that I will always be in your corner as you have been in mine. I don't understand it, but I know hate comes from all corners. I don't want to put you into any uncomfortable situations. When and if you are ready, you are welcome. I'll set you up. But I know we can continue to work together virtually. I'll be back here every so often, and I'm sure that you'll come when I need you. Again, I'm not giving you up."

"Thank you, Logan. This is what you need to do. I'm confident in this, and I'll be with you through your journey. I do expect to be the best man in your wedding, though or at least the ring bearer slash flower girl" I say, pulling out of the hug and wiping my eyes.

"That's a deal, although I think you are getting a little head of yourself," he says, laughing.

"Did you not pay attention to anything I've said?" I laugh. "I'm there for you both, no matter what."

"Thank you, Patrick. Means a lot." He pats me on the shoulder, and it seems awkward.

"That's what I do. Make sure I can't be replaced and forever in your debt."

"Well, you've succeeded, my friend," He says, laughing. "Looks like I have some planning to do. I'll need you fully on board for the next few days. You ready?"

"Born that way," I say, throwing my hand on my hip and jutting it out.

I don't want it to be a joke, but humor has always been my go-to. When in doubt, use humor. But sometimes it's not always funny for everyone involved. The only one not laughing right now is unfortunately me.

Chapter One

Patrick

I don't even know where to start. Do I start at the moment I met Buddy? Do I replay the hilarity of Mick and Marissa's wedding? Or do I start at the moment I watched the love of my life marry the love of his?

I'll start there, I guess. Even though I've been talking to William, or as all his friends call him, Buddy, for a while now, Logan's wedding is the first time we seem to be growing as a couple.

Logan had called me and told me about his proposal. I cried silently as I listened and also was so happy for him. It's a fucked up situation. A push and a pull of my heart. It's a wonder it's still beating.

Before he can ask me to be his best man, I tell him I want to be the ring bearer slash flower girl. He laughs and says, "only you, Patrick".

I would be more than honored to be his best man, but I can't see myself having to give that speech or standing shoulder to shoulder with him.

I want to go to my use of humor. My happy place.

Talking with William helps though. He has taken my mind off of Logan, that's for sure. I love when we video chat and I can see his animations. His accent is to die for. I've already discovered that he has several different sides. There is his professional side when I get him during his lunch hour and he's still in therapist mode. There's his friendly, sarcastic side that he shows to his friends when he's hanging out. Then there's my favorite side, the side where his voice lowers and he starts flirting and talking sexy.

I can tell that he is still not comfortable with showing that side to me. His face gets sort of flushed when I start flirting back. I still wonder if he really is gay.

His text messages are on fire though. He's much better with words in text form. He quickly has become my constant. Every morning we exchange messages and every night before he goes to sleep. The time difference is hard sometimes, but never a day goes by that we don't talk in some way.

I can't wait to get out there and see him in person again.

∞ ∞ ∞

It's the day of Logan and Presley Ann's wedding. We spent a lot of time making sure everything would be virtually impossible to see from even a helicopter. Not only is Logan one of the most eligible bachelors, and worth millions, his sister is also a recently retired supermodel.

So, a rental company put up a huge canopy to keep privacy and the paparazzi from being able to intrude. It may be big, but it's also very elegant.

The guys are all in the basement getting ready and Logan is pacing. I'm in my tux and I just put on a tutu. My little spin on being both the ring bearer and flower girl. Logan stops pacing and busts out laughing.

He pulls me away from everyone and says, "Patrick. Thank you, brother. I knew I could count on you to bring me back to reality. You're amazing, you know that right. You will make a wonderful husband one day. Sorry, it couldn't me."

I look at him in surprise, "How...did you know?"

"Dude, I may not be gay, but I knew. I can read people, remember? I also know that you are one of the strongest people I've ever known. I always suspected, but the day in my office when I told you I was moving, I could feel your sadness. I could tell you were trying so hard to be strong and not let on how you really felt. It killed me, dude. I never wanted to hurt you," he says.

"I know that. I know you would never hurt me. This is on me, Logan, not you. It is bittersweet. I love you and I always will, but I will turn it into brotherly love. I love Presley Ann and I love that you found her and will be happy. I can't wait for you to bring in some nieces or nephews for me to love upon. I would never jeopardize having you in my life. Even if it means I have to be on the sideline. It's better than not being there at all. I'll be okay, Logan. Let's get you married and make your happily ever after. Besides, I get to explore more with that mountain man this weekend," I say as he pulls me in for a hug.

The hug is strong and amazingly it helps me finally release everything. I hug him back just as strong and kiss his cheek. "Thank you, Logan. For always accepting me and making me feel like I mean something."

"You're not just my assistant, Patrick. You are my right-hand man, my brother. I don't know what I'd do without you. Seriously," he says pounding my back.

Our conversation is interrupted by the wedding planner who says it's time to take our positions. I take that as needing to get upstairs with the girls. Logan and I hug one last time and I watch as he heads up the steps.

I take in a deep cleansing breath, blowing it out as I look up and smile. I've got this.

I jog up two flights of stairs and open up the double doors leading into Logan and Presley Ann's master bedroom.

"Ladies. Who has my pillow and basket of flowers? Pattie boy is ready for duty," I announce to the room.

Presley Ann spins around and lets out a laugh, "You look amazing, Patrick! And thank you, you just helped calm my nerves a little."

"Well now that I know I have that effect on both you and Logan, I know you all won't get rid of me," I joke. "And you are the one who looks amazing. Girl, you are fine."

She's in a simple white sheath dress that molds to her curves. Her hair is braided to almost look like a halo. There are little baby breaths tucked in as well. Elegant and classy, yet down to earth and perfect.

"We love you, Patrick. You better never even think of leaving us," she says kissing my cheek. "How's Logan?"

"Nervous but dashingly handsome as always. The wedding coordinator just called them out, so are you ready?"

"I'm so ready. The ring pillow and the basket of petals are over there," she says pointing to a bench in front of their king size bed.

I look over the bed and wait for the pinch of pain, but instead, I just feel a little bump to the heart. It will get easier, I know.

I pick up the pillow and slide it on my wrist. There are fake rings tied to it. I lift the basket of petals and twirl around. "Let's get you married."

I made them all laugh again when it was my turn to walk down the aisle. I didn't walk though, I twirled and danced as I tossed petals in the air. I blew a few kisses to the ladies from Presley Ann's beauty parlor that I recognized. Then I stood stoic as vows and rings were exchanged. I wiped a few happy tears away when they were presented as husband and wife. I survived. I didn't crumble and die.

I caught Buddy's eyes on me sitting in the crowd. He smiled and my heart skipped. This time for good reasons. I smiled back and his grew larger. When he winks at me, I feel the butterflies stir.

At the reception, I find his table fairly quickly. He's with Missy Jo, but you can tell they are just friends. I can't stop looking at him to see if he's looking at me. Which he is most of the time. I find myself feeling giddy, and it's not from the champagne.

After dinner, I make my way over to the dessert table. I'm looking over all the deliciousness in front of me when a delicious little morsel comes and stands next to me.

"You were amazing today. Sorry, it took me so long to make it over to you. I really want to hug you right now, but it still doesn't feel safe," he says.

"It's okay. I completely understand. I'm more frustrated that I can't locate a damn buckeye on this table. It was my only request," I say putting my hands on my hips.

"Here," he says finding the plate full of the buckeyes I was looking for and handing me a few.

I pop one in my mouth and sigh, "Oh these are good. Nothing goes better together than chocolate and peanut butter." I lean into Buddy a little and whisper, "Well, almost."

He seems to get nervous and starts looking around.

"Can we get drinks and spend some time together," I say in order to give him time to calm down. I need to calm the old stallion down myself. The horse in my pants is trying to get out of the stable.

Once we get drinks, we find a table that is empty and away from the general crowd.

"I was so excited to actually see you again. How are you doing? I know that I need to behave and please tell me if I make you feel uncomfortable."

"It's okay. I'm sorry. I'm just not really good at this. You don't get a lot of practice when you are a demographic populous of one. Let's just say that I have to go into the city and most of the time, there is very little talking being done," Buddy says with a smirk. "Also, I'd like to see the more judgmental folks leave so I don't feel like I'm on guard."

"Just two friends catching up, nothing to see. I'll make sure there's a heterosexual amount of distance between us," I say trying to set him at ease. "I'm glad I don't have to worry about it as much where I live. There's still ignorance in some places, but for the most part, people don't even blink an eye."

"You are pretty amazing. I envy you. I mean, you came down that aisle with a fucking tutu on and no one seemed to even care. God forbid if I even thought of trying something like that. I get enough flack on the way I dress. I refuse to wear camo outside of hunting and that makes me weird around here. Also, my choice in hats is not of the ballcap variety. However, it's something that is me being true to at least that part of myself. Even if I have to hide the other part," he says downing his beer. "Need another one?" He points at my near empty glass as he stands.

"This is giving me heartburn. Get me the same as what you are drinking."

He comes back a few minutes later and hands me a bottle of beer. He taps his against it and says, "I'm excited to see you too, by the way."

"You seem a little more relaxed. Is it the beer?" I say laughing.

"It's the tutu. Definitely the tutu. How can anyone be nervous with a guy wearing one of those?" He says smiling back.

Man, I really like him. I never noticed how incredible his eyes were. He wears these black-rimmed glasses, so unless you are really close, they don't stand out. Right now, the way the light is hitting them, they just pop. They are an unusual shade of amber and I think I can see flecks of gold. I could get lost in them.

"I'd love for you to come to LA. I just happen to have access to a private jet. I mean, I'll have to get permission of course, but Logan loves me. I'm sure I'll be back here next month and maybe you can come back with me? Just a thought, no pressure," I say silently trying to send vibes his way.

"If you give me enough notice, it's doable. I've never been to LA," he says.

"Sounds like a plan. I'll let you know as soon as I know. You okay with getting home?" I ask seeing that it's getting late and people have dwindled down.

"Leaving me so soon?" he asks smiling.

"For now. I'm enjoying this, but I'm getting drunk and I think you are too. I want to make sure we get to know each other without letting it be testosterone driven. I'm so fucking attracted to you," I say being honest.

"Same and I agree. I need to find Missy Jo. She doesn't drink much and should be okay to get me home," he says looking around shaking my hand.

I look around as well and say, "Is there anyone here that will interpret a hug wrong?"

He gives me a bright smile and says, “Nah, I think it’s okay.”

We embrace and my heart starts to pound. The way his arms feel around me is amazing. When I feel his lips gently press against my neck, I feel my cock start to rise.

“Fuck, you need to stop. The chemistry is real and I would so take you home and fuck you right now. You made me so fucking hard with just a simple act of a kiss to the neck. You need to stop. Christ,” I say pulling away and trying to catch my breath.

“You make me feel special, Patrick. I’m dying inside here, but I understand. I want this to be different than all my other encounters. I just want you to know that the first time I saw you, I knew you were special. I had hoped to get to know you better. In fact, I prayed that I would. I’m going to go. Text or call me tomorrow, stallion,” he says with a little laugh and a shake of his head.

“Oh nicknames, huh? Okay, Doc,” I say smiling.

I watch him walk away and find myself smiling. Logan who?

Chapter Two

Buddy

He makes me laugh. I just love watching him. He's incredibly handsome and I admire how he just doesn't care what people think. I wish I could be more comfortable in my skin like he is. However, growing up in this town, I've seen firsthand the opinions concerning my lifestyle.

I am blessed that my mother is okay with it. She loves me and said she'll always love me, no matter what. When I came out to her, she said she wasn't really surprised. I used to play dress-up with her shoes and try to put makeup on. She told me it was a good thing my father was no longer with us. There would have been no way he would have accepted me.

I don't remember much about my father. He died of a massive heart attack when I was five. I received some death benefits that helped me with college. I'm still building my patient list but I'm partnering with other therapists that are older and more established than I am. When they get referred a younger patient that is struggling with their identity, or sexuality, they are immediately sent my way. I couldn't have done it on my own.

As soon as I get home, I send off a text to Patrick. I updated his contact name as stallion and it makes me laugh when I see it.

> **Me:** Made it home. Thank you for an amazing night of good conversation.
> **Stallion**: Glad you made it home safe. Loved seeing you in person.
> **Me:** Same. When are you heading back to LA?
> **Stallion:** I'm leaving Wednesday afternoon. Maybe we can get together tomorrow?
> **Me:** I would really like that. Goodnight, Stallion.
> **Stallion:** Goodnight, Doc.

I really like that he can be serious and not always a jokester, it's a side I want to explore more since I don't think he lets a lot of people see that side. Even though I really like his funny side, it's so refreshing.

In the morning, I call Missy Jo and tell her everything that happened last night. She's been an amazing friend and confidante in my life. She's always been my 'plus one' at any event, playing the girlfriend card for onlookers. I feel bad though, I feel like I'm holding her back from finding true love. She says she doesn't care, but I've always wondered if she felt more for me than just friends.

When we were younger, we dated and we were each other's first. It was the most uncomfortable thing I've ever experienced. I kept closing my eyes, trying to picture someone else. I knew then that I was definitely not into women. When I told her how I felt, she cried but said she knew. She vowed then to always protect me and be there for me as long as I needed her.

I know that she's passed on dates because of me. I don't like that at all. I also know that there is a guy in her office that keeps asking her out.

"Missy Jo, I really want you to go out with Jason. I don't want to hold you back from finding love. It's not fair. I love you, with all my heart and you have been such a Godsend to me, but it's your time now. For me, please?" I beg.

"I had a feeling that things were going to change this weekend, so when he asked me out yesterday, I agreed. We are going to dinner tomorrow," she says.

"Oh, Missy Jo, that's wonderful. I'm so excited for you. You need to let me know how it goes," I say excitedly.

"You need to let me know how things go with Patrick. I'm so happy for you. This is big, Buddy. This is your time to finally explore a real relationship and not those stupid hookups you used to do," Missy Jo says.

"Love you, girl," I say as my heartbeat speeds at the possibilities.

"Love you too, Buddy," she responds.

As soon as I hang up, I get a call from Mick asking to meet me for lunch. As soon as I agree, my phone rings.

"Hey, Patrick. I just got a call from Mick wanting to have lunch," I say immediately as I answer.

"Yeah, funny thing. I just got a call from Marissa asking me to go to lunch. I think we are getting ambushed. Are you okay with this?" he asks.

"Mick is one of my best friends. I wish I could have come out to him a long time ago. I think this is my chance to just come clean and play my cards. I don't want to lose him as a friend, but I need to start being honest. This isn't going to be easy," I say.

"What do you want me to say? I'm going to take your lead here. I don't want to make anything uncomfortable for you. I really want to explore things with you. We have mutual friends and it would be easier on you if you had a support system back here. So, we can continue to explore us and figure out things," he says.

"Be honest. I want to explore things with you too. I agree that it would be so much easier for me if my inner circle finally knew. I could at least stop hiding this side of me from them. I'm nervous as fuck, but I think I need this," I respond.

"Okay. I think it will be good. Mick and Marissa will be in our corner. I truly feel that it's going to be okay," he says.

"Call me after and let me know how it goes," I say.

"Of course, you will be my first call," he says as he hangs up.

I head out to the diner and immediately see Mick. I take a seat and just dive right in.

"So, what's up? I know we are friends and all but meeting up for lunch isn't something we normally do," I say as I sit down.

"Busted," Mick says shrugging his shoulders. "Okay, don't hit me or get mad. I'm clueless about these things and I don't really even know how to say it other than just saying it," He ends as he fidgets with the menu.

I reach out and push my hand down on the menu to stop his movements, "Yes, Mick. I am."

"How do you know what I'm going to say?" he says meeting my eyes with questions.

I smile and say, "Patrick texted me that he was meeting Marissa for lunch. Once I told him I was meeting you for lunch, we kinda figured you all were going to ask, and play matchmaker or whatever."

"Huh, wow. You're smarter than I thought," he says pulling the menu from under my hand. "I'm starving. Where the hell is our waitress."

"That's it? That's all you have to say? We've been friends forever and I just come out to you and you act like it's nothing." I say crossing my arms.

"Because it is nothing, Bud. Love who you want to love. None of my business as long as my friends are happy. Or maybe I need to say, congratulations on liking butt sex? I like a little finger action there myself. I guess Patrick is okay looking, for a guy. Wait, is crossing your arms like that the same as it is with Marissa? Should I take cover?" he asks leaning back a little.

I drop my arms and start laughing. "No, I'm just surprised is all. I guess I thought you'd give me a hard time or not want to be my friend anymore," I say waving over the waitress. "Can you take our order before my friend wastes away to nothing?"

We order and fall into our normal kind of interaction. After lunch as we are walking to our trucks. I pull Mick in for a hug. "Be careful of that finger action, you know that's the same thing they say about marijuana, it's the gateway drug to becoming gay," I say with a smirk.

"Shut up asshole. We all know marijuana's not a gateway drug. Neither is a little finger. If it feels good, I say do it," he responds laughing.

"Of course, I'm teasing. Thank you though. I was really worried about losing you as a friend," I say.

"You'll always be my friend, shit man. Come over tomorrow night. Patrick will be heading back and we want to have a little bonfire. Just us," Mick says patting my back.

"Awesome. It'll be nice to not be in hiding as much. I'm looking forward to it. Thank you," I say pulling away and fixing my fedora. "Thanks again. You know you are my favorite friend, right?"

"Of course, I am. Why wouldn't I be?" he says laughing.

I sent Patrick off a text asking how his lunch went and immediately my phone rings.

"So, Marissa was all sweet asking about you and wanting us to come over tomorrow night. She saw us together and now is wanting to do everything she can to make a love connection. Bless her heart," Patrick says laughing. "How did it go with you and Mick?"

"I was honest, and I came out to Mick. He was amazing actually and I wish I would have done it a long time ago. I'm looking forward to hanging out tomorrow night and seeing you," I say.

"Me too, Doc. What are you doing tonight though? Wanna come over and hang out at the hotel bar?" he asks with a song in his voice.

"I would love too, but I have early patients. I do paperwork on Tuesday and usually do that from home. It's the only reason I agreed to meet tomorrow night. I'm sorry," I say feeling bad.

"No, it's alright. I never asked if you have your own place or not," Patrick says.

"Yeah, I have a bachelor pad. I actually live in a townhouse right behind the shopping plaza. I'm saving up to build on a plot of land I'm paying for right now. Why?" I ask.

"I don't want to rush anything, but fuck I'm bored. Can I come over to you and just chill? I promise not to stay late or take advantage of you," he asks and I can almost see him pouting.

"I'd like that. I'll cook you dinner. You can pick out a movie and I'll judge our future on your choice," I say teasing.

"Well, this kinda sucks, dude. I don't really know that much about you to know if I fuck up," he says. "But challenge accepted I guess."

"There you go. Way to step up. I'll text you my address. Say around six?" I ask.

"I'll be there. See you later, Doc," he says.

Chapter Three

Patrick

I'm so excited that I'm going to see him tonight. I keep telling myself that I need to behave and I just need to go and hang out and get to know him better.

I knew Mick was amazing. He's always handled my gay jokes like a champ. I'm so happy that it all seemed to work out. Plus, he's cooking for me. How amazing is that? The last time I had anything homemade was the last time I was here. I remember it being amazing, and I had to work out for a full week to get the weight off that I gained.

I'm not a big guy. But, I can say that I can get a beer belly real quick if I don't watch it. I can be vain and one of the things I pride myself on is my lean body. I also have tattoos hidden under my dress shirts that most people never see.

I search through my clothes and they're mostly all designer. I really want to just dress down and normal. I find a pair of distressed jeans and my favorite old t-shirt that I normally work out in. I know Buddy normally dresses pretty fly, but I'm hoping when he's at home, he's relaxed.

I tap in the address and hop into my rental. I head out and I try to get out of my head. This is going to be good. It's going to be fantastic.

I've reached my destination and it's cute. It's small, but it's cute. I pull next to his truck and take a deep breath. I just want this to go well.

I shake off my nerves and exit my car. As I pop up to the door, it opens and I'm greeted with an amazing smile. He's in distressed jeans and a t-shirt as well. His feet are bare and he looks so relaxed.

"Hey Doc," I say.

"Hey, handsome. So happy you're here," he says with a huge smile.

He steps aside and I walk in and see an amazing home. It feels instantly comfortable. I smell something amazing and smile.

"So, what's on the menu, Doc?" I ask.

"Chicken Alfredo. Hope that's okay. I know you fit guys don't normally do carbs, but it's my specialty," he responds.

"I love it. I'll just have to work out harder for the rest of the week. Gotta keep up these abs," I say, pointing to my midsection.

He surprises me by coming up to me and pressing his hands against my abs, "Incredible abs from what I could see by stalking you on social media."

"That's dangerous, Doc. Just saying. I told you I was going to behave but having your hands on me shoots all my good intentions out of the window," I say trying not to grab him and pull him into me.

"Let's eat and then talk," he says backing away and leading me into the kitchen.

We sit down at a simple table that has one single candle lit. I feel his feet intertwine with mine and I feel myself getting hard. This is not going to be innocent and he only has himself to blame. I dig in and it's fucking amazing.

"Holy shit, Doc. This is so good," I say.

"So, tell me about your family. You say you don't know me, but I think I know less about you," he says as he twirls some noodles and takes a big bite.

"It's actually not what you may think. I didn't come out until after I graduated from college and I haven't spoken to my parents since. They were not happy at all. It was bad. If it wouldn't have been for my job that I landed with Logan I would have given up. He never judged me and to be honest, I fell in love with him. Stupid, I know. I want to be honest though. Sometimes our feelings are out of our control. He was my rock that helped me move on. I knew that we would never be together, but it was something that I fantasized about and it helped me," I say tucking my head.

"Logan is fucking hot. I don't blame you. You know that it wasn't real though, right? I may have had my share of the unreal. Even worse being in this town," he says reaching out and lifting my chin.

"Oh, I knew it would never happen. It was stupid. It was also really hard when he told me he was moving away and going to propose to Presley Ann. Thank God I love her as much as I do. She's incredible and I really am happy for him. My little fantasy bubble burst, and I was really sad for a while. I know there is someone out there for me. I want to find him. I don't want to look too far into the future or get too consumed, but I feel something when I look at you. I don't want to scare you either. However, I don't want to miss the chance of meeting my forever. Heart be damned," I say feeling like I've overexposed myself.

"Honestly. The first time you came into town, I was intrigued. I want to find out too. You make me laugh, you have a powerful presence and I want to find out more. I want to jump in and just try. There will be times where I will pull away. Only because I'm scared of people finding out here. Please talk to me if I get weird," he says setting down his fork.

"Nothing weird, if I can help it. I like you. I want to explore the possibilities. If you are in, so am I," I say grabbing his hand.

"I'm in," he says squeezing my hand and smiling.

"This is really good, Doc. Are you sure you aren't a chef too?" I joke.

"No, not a chef, but I can handle my own in the kitchen," he says laughing.

"Can you handle me in the kitchen?" I say feeling a little frisky.

"I thought we were going to behave," he says smiling.

"Honest, we are. Eat and let me try to pick out a movie that will decide our fate," I say smiling.

We finished eating and I feel like I'm on carb overload. We walk to the couch and he turns on the TV and brings up the movie app. I sit down beside him and hold out my hand for him to hand over the remote.

Chapter Four

Buddy

It really doesn't matter what he picks. I'm probably not going to even watch. My heart is beating hard and I'm trying to stay calm. I've never had the opportunity to even consider a long term relationship with the men I've been with. It has always been known upfront that it was just sex. This is different and I don't want to mess anything up.

I hand him the remote and watch his face as his expression changes as he looks over my viewed library. "You have a real variety of interests here, dude."

"Adds to the mystery," I tease.

"Well, I've seen this a thousand times, but let's see what you think. Now the test goes back to you. Because, if you do not like this, we cannot be friends," he jokes as he queues up his choice.

"As you wish," I say laughing.

"Oh damn, yes. We can be friends," he says as I position myself into the corner of my couch, lifting my leg up and stretching out.

Smiling, he positions himself in front of me. His back to my front, my leg up over his. I wrap my arms around his middle as he wraps his arms on top of mine.

"Are you being alpha, Doc," he says squeezing my arms.

"My turf, I tend to be more dominant. Are you okay with that?" I ask.

"Oh, yeah. I'm definitely okay with that," he says relaxing his body against mine.

I laugh as I listen to him quote the movie word for word. I know it, but obviously, he really knows it. He gets animated at parts and I find myself loving the movie even more than I had before.

"As you wish means so much more to me now. What do you wish?" I ask tilting my head down and nuzzling into his neck.

I feel him take in a deep breath and say. "I wish to spend more times like this with you."

He leans forward and turns his upper body to face me. We lock eyes and it just feels natural. The next step is to kiss him. I look at his lips as he looks at mine. We lean in slow.

The first kiss. People don't put a lot of value on that. I do. The first kiss is the moment you will know. That moment where you will either feel it or you won't. If it's too wet, too much, I'm done. But when our lips meet, it's more than perfect. I feel it consume me. I can only picture kissing this man for the rest of my life. It's soft and tender and just perfect.

Our kissing gets stronger and more intense. He turns on his knees and takes my face into his hands. Even as we get more intense, it's still perfect. I slow it down and take a deep breath and press my forehead against his.

"Wow," It's all I can say at this point.

"Perfect," he responds. "I think we need to stop and I need to go. I don't want to ruin this moment."

"I agree. Thank you. I can't wait to see what tomorrow brings," I say giving him one last peck as we get up and I walk him to the door.

"See you tomorrow, Doc," he says as he gives me one last hug.

I watch as he gets into his car and blows me a kiss and I can't help but laugh. I blow a kiss back and lean against the door frame pressing my fingers to my lips. I don't want to get ahead of myself, but I think I'm watching my forever drive down my driveway.

Chapter Five

Patrick

Buddy picks me up and we head over to Mick and Marissa's. We are all sitting around a bonfire and it just feels comfortable. Buddy is holding my hand and we exchange smiles back and forth. He seems so much lighter and relaxed. He needed this more than anyone may have realized.

Mick and Marissa keep smiling at us and it feels wonderful.

We make small talk and cook smores. Mick catches his marshmallows on fire every time and makes Marissa blow them out.

"Babe, do you like them burnt?" she asks.

"Actually, I do, but I like to watch your lips even more," he says making her laugh.

"Still in the honeymoon phase, I see," I say.

"Hopefully we never leave it. I think the nice thing is we moved a little faster than most and are still learning about each other. Some may think it's crazy and maybe we might discover things we don't like about each other. I don't think that will ever happen, though. I mean we can already laugh at each other. I honestly believe that humor is very important in a relationship," Mick answers.

"Well, thank God Patrick is funny then," Buddy says, smiling.

"I'm fucking hilarious, babe. Truthfully though, I can be a bit flamboyant at times. I can't help it. It's just me, though," I say, waving my hands around. "But this guy right here, he is one of the most sarcastic people I've ever met. It's quite funny."

"So, Buddy. I really don't know much about you. Tell me a little about yourself," Marissa asks.

"Well, what most people don't know is my real name is William. I'm twenty-eight with a doctorate in psychology, and I'm a therapist with a practice in Knoxville. I focus on sexuality and gender themed topics, along with the common things such as depression and anxiety," Buddy says. "I'm known as Buddy around here, and even though it might sound like I'm successful, I'm a good ol' country boy at heart. I love the mountains and the simple things in life. Oh, and beer. I really like beer."

“Wow don’t take this wrong, but I would have never thought you were a doctor. Impressive. Oh my God! Do you think you could be a counselor or someone to help if needed at my safe house? I don’t mean to come right at you, but if you can’t, maybe you can recommend someone? This is exciting,” Marissa says, jumping up and squeezing between us.

“Well now, don’t mind me,” I say, getting up and moving to where she was sitting.

“Absolutely. I think it’s wonderful what you are doing,” Buddy says.

“So, I don’t mean to get personal, but how did you manage to hide the fact that you were gay from even Mick?” Marissa asks. “I mean, not that it’s anyone’s business but your own, but your friends are there to support you.”

“Have you seen my friends? I mean, I guess I should have known that Mick would have been okay, but you just don’t know, and I was scared of being labeled or looked at differently. My momma knows. I guess the fact that I wanted to play dress-up with her shoes and play with dolls growing up was a clear sign. I always dressed differently. She’s been my rock. But I also love to hunt. I’m still a man. I just like other men. This town is small, and I really didn’t want to hurt my momma either. I overheard one of her best friends talking bad about same-sex marriages and I vowed to keep it away from affecting her. It may seem cowardly but it's just easier.

"Missy Jo and I would probably be married in a few years with a couple of kids if Patrick wouldn't have come along. I truly love that girl. I realize that I was holding her back. I wasn't being fair to myself or her. She's been super supportive, but I know I hurt her."

I get up and walk over and pull him up. "You are so incredibly strong. I was so pissed at Logan for springing this sabbatical on me and look at what happened. Love in these damn Smokies with me meeting an incredible guy when I least expected it. Who knew? A sexy doctor, too. It's been tough, though, hiding. I'm not used to having to hide. I respect William and his choices. Yes, damn you all, I refuse to call him Buddy. He's my William."

"It's a beautiful love snowball rolling across the Smokies," Marissa says, jumping up and throwing her arms around us.

"Oh, hell. Y'all are killing me!" Mick says, getting up and coming over and joining into the embrace.

We ended the evening laughing, eating more smores, and getting to talk openly and honestly. I feel closer to all of them afterwards.

I'm scared though. I feel like I can jump in with both feet but I feel like this is all new for him. I think I need to hit the pause button or something. I think we can go the distance and I don't want it to end before it begins.

I also don't want him to think I'm pulling away either. I just want to make sure that I don't scare him off.

We say our goodbyes and walk out to his truck. Once we are both in the cab, he leans towards me and says, "So is it going to be William or Doc? You know, no one here will know who you are referring to with either of those."

"All the better. I don't want to keep you a secret, but I understand. I want you to be comfortable. I'll call you Buddy when around your friends, I'll call you William when we are intimate, and I'll call you Doc all the other times," I say.

"You have it all figured out," he says with a weak smile.

"No, I don't. I don't have anything figured out. I'm just as confused as you and I want to make sure you are okay. I know this isn't what you are used to and honestly, I don't want you to get scared and run. I think we need to step back and take our time with this. I don't even know if you take or give," I say smirking.

"I want this too, Patrick. I'm good with slowing down to make sure we get to know each other. As for what I like, I'm more dominant and tend to take control. So, beware of that. But please don't hold back. I want to go all in and see where it goes. Heart be damned, but I really think we have something here," he says leaning over and pressing his lips to mine.

It's simple and sweet, but again I feel it.

"What do you feel when we are together?" I ask.

"I feel home," he says leaning his head back against the car headrest. "I don't want it to end."

"So, we won't let it. Let's just go day by day and grow together. We will see where it leads, okay?" I say rubbing his arm.

"Okay," he says. "I can't wait to find out where we go with this."

Chapter Six

Buddy

I take the long way back to his hotel. I don't want this night to end. He's leaving tomorrow and I'm not sure when I will get to see him again.

"I've only been here a few times, but I'm pretty sure it doesn't take this long to get to the hotel. Are you stalling, Doc?" he says as he squeezes my hand.

"Busted. I just don't want this night to end," I say trying to hold back my emotions.

"Then why does it have to?" he says seemingly shy.

"Are you getting shy on me? I can't have you getting shy on me. Do you want this night to end or are you going to invite me up to your hotel room when we get there?" I say pulling out my alpha card.

"You tell me," he says.

I pull his hand up to my mouth and nibble on his knuckles. "You are mine tonight. Do you think you are ready for me?"

"I'm yours to do what you wish," he says with a slight chuckle.

"Oh, we are going there? As you wish?" I say getting a bit nervous myself.

I pull into the parking lot and we exit the truck and start towards the lobby. I stop dead in my tracks as I recognize the person at the front desk.

Patrick notices me stopping and turns to ask, "What's wrong, Doc?"

"Is there a side entrance?" I say taking a deep breath and questioning why I'm even here.

Patrick steps in front of me and seems to understand immediately. "Hey, look at me. We don't have to do this, but I want you so bad. I don't want you to feel uncomfortable. We won't have a good experience if you are tense. That would totally ruin the mood."

I laugh and shake out my hands. "I'm so sorry. I'm okay. I just would rather not go through the lobby."

"Okay. Follow me," Patrick says taking off in a jog to the side of the hotel.

I feel like a teenager trying to sneak around and get away with something from my parents.

I start laughing as I chase him around the hotel to a side entrance. Once I catch up to him, he has the side door open and is bowed over like he is welcoming me into the door. I walk in as he follows behind.

"I'm on the first floor actually. I didn't even think about it, I'm sorry. Right ahead two doors." He says.

"I'm sorry for making you feel like we have to sneak around," I say walking towards the room.

"Doc, It's okay. I understand," he says as he swipes his keycard.

As soon as we get into the room, my dominant side takes over. I'm so fucking hard and I want him so bad. I end up pushing him against the door as it closes and toss my fedora across the room.

My chest is heaving against him and his is against mine as I stare into his eyes and glance down to his lips. He licks his bottom lip and I'm done.

I grab his chin and dive in. As soon as our lips meet, I lose all control. His mouth is divine, and I want more. I feel his hands drop to my pants and start undoing them. I spin us around and start to walk us over to the bed.

He drops to the bed and looks up at me and smiles. God, I love his smile. I feel like I'm going to explode. I take a deep breath as he pushes my jeans down and they drop to the floor. My cock springs free and slaps against my stomach and I let out a groan.

"Commando, me like," Patrick says as he takes my cock in his hand and gives it a stroke. I step in closer and take his face into my hands, guiding him to where I want him.

"Suck me," I grunt.

Without hesitation, Patrick takes my cock into his hands and presses it against my stomach He leans down and runs his tongue over my balls. He sucks them one by one into his mouth and I'm pulsating. Running his tongue up my shaft, he never takes his eyes off of me and it's the sexiest thing I've ever seen.

"Fuck yes," I barely get out as he reaches the tip and wraps his lips around me.

I grab the back of his head as he takes me into his mouth. He fucking deep throats me and I almost lose it.

"Stop. Fuck," I yell.

Patrick stops and takes off his shirt and pants and scoots back onto the bed. I see firsthand the tattoos that I've seen on his social media. Seeing them in person, I'm so turned on.

"Fuck, you are beautiful." I say taking off my shirt and my glasses and crawl up the bed.

Patrick rolls to the side and grabs a condom. Leaning up I grab the condom and smile. "Stay the way you are."

"Okay, how's this going to work?" he says watching as I put the condom on.

I grab his legs and pull him down the bed as I spread them wide and press them up into his armpits.

"So intimate," He says as he hands me lube that seemed to come out of nowhere. Putting a little on a finger, I rub the rim slowly pressing it into his ass feeling him grip my finger. My cock jumps with anticipation. I rub the rest on my wrapped cock and lean forward to take his lips.

He meets my kisses without hesitation as I look straight into his eyes. "You know you are mine. This just makes it more real."

I press forward and enter him slowly. That first breach is the most surreal. Once I'm in, it's heaven. I see his eyes dilate as his mouth forms an "o". I can feel his cock jump against my stomach. I reach between us and grab him. The groan he lets out is amazing.

I move my arms behind his knees and get leverage. "You ready?" I say as I spread my knees and look directly into his eyes.

"Fuck me, William," he says.

I lost myself at that moment. I thrust forward as I pull him towards me. Our eyes never waver. As I thrust forward, I see his pleasure, as I feel mine.

His legs wrap around my back and encourage me forward. "I'm going to cum." I say.

"Fuck it feels so good, don't stop," he says as he reaches between us and starts stroking himself.

I feel the tingling in my balls and I feel the wetness of his release and that's all it takes. I yell out as I release and pull him close.

I fall into him and can't seem to catch my breath. "That was incredible," he says engulfing me in his arms.

I'm done. I've never felt this way after sex. I can feel a part of me getting lost in Patrick.

"I'm consumed by you, Patrick." I say as I pull out and roll over and let out a breath. I grab a tissue off the nightstand and dispose of the condom.

He rolls into me and wraps his arms around me. "I've never been taken that way. That was amazing and you are right, it was so much more intimate. You're going to make me fall for you, William."

"I'm feeling emotions that I have never felt before. I don't know what it all means. It's a little overwhelming," I say taking a deep breath and rub his arm.

"We have time. There isn't a ticking clock here. I'll be committed to you and I look forward to growing this relationship. If you are, that is," he says reaching out and rubbing my face.

"I definitely am. I've never done a long distance relationship before. How's this going to work?" I ask.

"I've never done long distance either. So, we take one day at a time, just like any other relationship. Except we are on different sides of the continent. We have phones, real time video calls that will make it seem like we are in the same room. "It won't be easy, but I think it will be worth it," he says letting out a sigh.

"I think so, too, Patrick. Damn. Your tattoos are badass and sexy as fuck," I say as I sit up and look over the artwork on his body. He has a full sleeve on his left arm. His peck has a shield with a lion. I find myself tracing them and I notice his arms break out with goose pimples. I run my fingers up and over his shoulder that has what looks like armor and run them over the shield on his chest. I see his nipple get hard and I can't help but lean over and take it into my mouth. He sucks in a breath as I nibble with my teeth and flick it with my tongue.

The next thing I know, I'm flipped over to the middle of the bed and Patrick has me pinned. "Fuck, you turn me on so bad. Have you ever been bottom?"

"No, and I'm not sure I'm ready for that," I say honestly.

"I respect that. We will work up to it if we can?" he says smiling and giving me a kiss.

He moves to the center of the bed and pulls me up. He extends his legs around me and lifts my legs over his. We are almost chest to chest. What I did earlier was new to him and this is totally new to me. I tilt my head in question as he smiles and takes both of our cocks into his hands. He presses his forehead against mine and rubs our cocks together and it feels incredible.

I reach up and grab his neck and pull his face to mine and our lips meet softly at first. He mimics me by holding my neck and I mimic him as I wrap my fingers around his and join in with rubbing our cocks.

Our movements increase and our kiss gets more intense. I love the softness of his lips but the roughness of his stubble.... my toes start to curl as I feel the rush of my orgasm starting.

My grip on our cocks gets tighter as does his grip on my neck. We both gasp into each other's mouth. We both stop kissing and look down to watch as we each release streams of cum. We cover each other and I can't help but continue to rub my cock against his and join us together.

"Fuck," he says as he lays back on the bed and letting go. I do the same and smile.

"You may have not had my ass, but that was a first for me, so we both sort of had our firsts tonight," I say rubbing his legs.

"You just rubbed cum all over my legs, dude," he says laughing.

"Yeah, well, I'm okay with that. Guess we need to take a shower then," I say laughing.

"Quick one. I'm exhausted," he says getting up and staggering to the bathroom. "Damn, I feel like I'm drunk."

We take a shower together and it's nice and comforting and feels so natural. We dry off in silence and walk to the bed together. We both crawl under the covers and fold into one another.

"I'll drive you to the airport tomorrow," I say as he gives me a soft kiss.

"Okay. Goodnight, Doc," he says as his body relaxes around me.

I've never actually slept in a bed with another man. I can't believe how incredible it feels. I find myself fading off quickly as I hear Patrick's breathing slow. I slowly fall asleep myself with a smile on my face.

With a man wrapped around me and his soft breathing in my ear, I feel like I've never felt before. A total sense of belonging.

Chapter Seven

Patrick

You would think with the time difference, I would still be sleeping. As soon as the sun shone through the window, I was wide awake. I feel like I need to take a run or something. I really shouldn't have all this energy this early in the morning.

I glance at Buddy sleeping soundly as I pack up my bags, setting out a change of clothes that I'll be traveling in. He's stretched out on his stomach with his hands tucked under his pillow. There's just a sheet covering his ass and legs. His back is bare, and I trace the sinewed shape of his shoulders with my eyes. He's lean yet defined. There are a lot of similarities between us. The biggest difference is his skin is an empty canvas.

You can tell by the tone that he isn't afraid of the sun. I can almost see the line where his tan stops at the top of his ass cheek. It's hiding under the sheet.

I fold my clothes and place them inside my suitcase without taking my eyes off of him trying to embed the image to memory. I don't have to leave. I mean my boss is on his honeymoon, after all.

My mind starts to wander at how I can possibly change plans and stay a few days longer, just as my phone starts to ring.

Buddy pulls the pillow over his head and groans as I rush to get the ringing phone off the dresser.

I slip in the bathroom to take the call. It's from one of the construction managers. I guess I will need to go home now. He goes on to tell me that they continue to have problems with things going missing from the site.

I let him know that I will get someone to hire security for overnights and end the call. Logan is going to need another assistant for all of his ventures. I'm starting to run ragged trying to keep everything in check these days.

I place a call to the head of operations and pass on the responsibility to him to take care of the situation. I need to start delegating shit or I'm going to lose my own shit.

I quickly brush my teeth and throw my bathroom shit in my toiletry bag.

I walk back out into the room and sit down at the desk to boot up my laptop. I respond to a few emails and forward others on to start my task of delegation.

I send off a text to check in with Smitty to see when he plans on getting here and when I need to be at the airport. I'm engrossed in what I'm doing so when two hands settle on my shoulders, I jump.

"Easy there, tiger," Buddy says as he massages my muscles.

I lean my head back into his stomach and look up at him. "Scared the shit out of me. Mmm, that feels good."

His hair is disheveled, but he looks sexy as he looks down at me with a smirk. He looks around and his soft smile fads. "Looks like you are all packed."

"Yeah, I'm waiting to hear from the pilot on when he's supposed to be here. I don't want to go," I say as I close my laptop and look down.

Buddy runs his hands down my chest, leaning over me and pulling me against him tight.

"I don't want you to leave, either. I'm going to miss you," he says softly.

I fold my arms over his and sigh, "Sucks."

"Yes, please," he says standing up straight and spinning my chair around.

"You need to be careful with that thing. You almost took my eye out," I say when I see him fully hard and naked before me.

He swings his hips back and forth making his cock move from side to side. "You wanna sword fight or what?" he says laughing.

I stand, drop my boxers and take my cock in my hand giving it a few strokes. "Touché."

I laugh as he mimics me and taps the head of his against mine. We pretend sword fight for a few minutes, chasing each other around the room until we are both out of breath.

"I surrender," I say raising my hands over my head.

"I like those words coming from your lips," he says spinning me around and walking me over to the wall next to the bed. "Assume the position."

"Yes, sir," I say smiling as I press my hands against the wall and smile at him over my shoulder.

"Spread, 'em," he says tapping my foot until I'm almost spread eagle.

I hear the ripping of the condom and my heart rate starts to speed. I feel his hands start to roam all over my body as he leans in and sucks the tender spot right under my ear.

"You have an amazing body, Patrick," he says as he continues to trace his fingers over my back.

His touch is tender and soft, running up my arms, back down and over my shoulders. My cock jerks as he continues down to caress my ass cheeks, spreading them and placing his cock in between. I capture his shaft and squeeze as he thrusts up and down with a groan.

His hands circle my hips and run up my stomach to my chest. With a small pinch of my nipples, I throw my head back and moan, "Fuck, William."

"I love hearing you say my name," he says as he slowly runs his hands back down. He is grinding himself up and down as he bites down on my collar bone and shoulder.

Once his one hand reaches my cock, he pushes his other hand between my shoulder blades pushing me down, so I have to bend at the waist.

He twists as he reaches back to get the lube and I groan with anticipation. With lube on both hands, I feel him rubbing it on him as he brushes against my ass. He reaches around, grabbing my balls, giving them a little tug and then wraps his fingers around my shaft.

As he continues to stroke me, I feel him teasing my opening. I let out a breath and try to relax as he pushes forward. That first tinge of pain as he breaches quickly disappears with pleasure. There's a spot he hits that has me seeing stars.

He continues to stoke me as he thrusts up inside making my toes curl. I move one hand off the wall and take over stroking myself. He moves his hands to my hips and increases his speed to the point I'm finding it difficult to keep from hitting my head against the wall.

"Fuck, fuck, fuck," I groan with each hard push.

He moans as his movements become long and deep. "Don't come until I tell you to."

I can feel the veins in my neck pop as I strain to hold back, "I'm gonna blow, please."

With one hard slap to my ass, he yells, "Fuck, yes. Come Patrick."

I feel like I'm going to blackout as the pleasure seems to expel from my body in long spurts onto the wall. I have a hard time catching my breath as I lean my arms and cheek against the wall.

He slows his movements but continues to move in and out of me. I can feel his cock pulse as he seems to continue to come. With one last thrust up, he grinds against me and shakes as he growls deep.

He presses fully against me, running his hands up my arms and intertwines his fingers with mine. I feel his labored breathing against me as he softly kisses my cheek.

"Let's take a shower," he says, still using his alpha tone.

"I vote for a bubble bath, but that's just me," I say as I feel him start to chuckle behind me.

∞ ∞ ∞

The one thing nice about using a private jet, you have a private entrance and can pull right up onto the tarmac. I see the steward standing at the bottom of the steps waiting for the truck to stop.

"I always feel so special when I take Logan's plane. They don't care that I'm just a personal assistant. It's pretty awesome, really," I say.

“I wouldn’t know how to even act,” Buddy says pulling the truck to a stop.

“I never get used to it. But I do love it. I’m a queen, after all,” I say trying to keep a happy mood.

“When are you coming back?” he asks pressing his lips together and looking away from me.

“Hey, look at me,” I say turning towards him in the truck.

He sucks in a deep breath and I watch as he wipes his eyes under his glasses. He turns to me and tries to smile.

I wiggle my fingers, reaching out for his hands. Once I have them, I pull them to my lips, giving his knuckles a kiss. “It will pass faster than we think. I’ll be back soon, or I’ll have you out there to see me. This is just the beginning. It sucks, I know, but as I said before, I’m committed.”

“I’m committed too, and I’m sorry for getting emotional. I just really enjoy being with you and what we have started. It makes me sad that you are leaving,” he says as a tear rolls down his eye.

“Fuck, babe. You’re killing me. You can be all manly and shit and yet show your vulnerable side. You’re everything I could have hoped to have found to be a part of my life. It’s going to be a hell of a journey and it's only the beginning," I say leaning forward and giving him a kiss.

Our kiss deepens and we both grab the back of each other's necks. We end with our foreheads pressed together. "Until next time, Doc."

"I can't wait," he says laughing through a few tears.

We give each other one last kiss as I exit the truck and wipe my tears as I walk up the plane stairs. I turn before heading in and blow him a kiss. I watch as he pretends to catch it and press his hand against his chest.

I send off a text before we take flight, "You have my heart."

When I land, I see a message back from him, "You have mine."

Chapter Eight

Buddy

I stay and watch as the plane takes off and I don't leave until I can no longer see it. I miss him already.

I decide to go over and visit my momma. I need someone to ground me and she always knows how to do it.

I pull into the driveway and my momma is sitting on her front porch wearing a huge smile and drinking what I know is her favorite sweet tea.

"Just made a fresh batch, go on and grab yourself some and come sit with me for a while," she says raising her glass.

I go inside and walk back to the kitchen and grab myself a glass of tea. I see that she also made a batch of chocolate chips cookies. I grab a plate and put a few on it and take them outside with me.

"Presley Ann looked beautiful and her man, whoo wee, he is a good looking feller," she says grabbing a cookie and taking a bite.

"Momma, you ol' cougar. He's too young for you," I say laughing.

"I'm only fifty-one, my rule is if I can't have given birth to them, they are not off limits. And hey, I'm not dead. I've even signed up for one of those old people dating sites," she smiles.

"Gross, but cool. I'm torn here ma. I mean, I never understood why you stayed single. You deserve to be happy too. Any prospects?" I say trying not to think about my momma dating.

"Not yet. I mean, I don't think I look my age and I know I'm not perfect, but yesh, these men are something. They look like they've lived a very hard life. None are smiling, so I can only assume they don't have all their teeth. Even though I joke about age, I don't feel right about going too young. I think I may just hang out at the grocery store and hope to find a Logan, like Presley Ann did," she says getting a silly smile on her face.

"I think that was one in a million, ma," I say laughing.

"Well a woman can only hope," she says with a sigh. "So, tell me about this Patrick guy."

"What do you mean?" I say trying to play dumb.

"Oh, don't try to play innocent with me. I saw you and I know you, baby. He's quite handsome. Tell me about him," she says.

I lean back and smile, "He's incredible ma. I can totally see a forever with him. I'm scared though. He's all the way on the other side of the country. How would this even work?"

"It will work because you care about each other and there is so much technology out there that it won't seem like you are even that far apart. He'll be out here often, right? And you can go out there as well. It will be okay. I believe that love conquers all. Who knows, maybe he can change a few people's minds out here. The girls at the beauty parlor love him. I'm not sure they understand though. They can't be that stupid though. I just want the best for you and I want you to be able to live your life without ridicule. I love you baby, and I want you to be happy. These narrowed minded people just piss me off. One day. One day, I'm gonna raise my sweet tea and shout from my porch that my son is gay and everyone can just go fuck themselves," she says taking a drink.

"I don't want you to have any issues, ma," I say.

"William, you do not worry about me. You do NOT worry about what I may encounter. I can handle myself. I love you. I want you to be happy and I'll be damned if anyone will tell me that what you are doing is wrong. Do not hold back from doing this because of me. All my friends can fuck themselves if they have anything negative to say. I don't want them as friends if that is even the case. Baby, I love you," she says wiping her eyes.

"Momma, don't. I can't handle you crying because of me," I say reaching out for her hand.

"You stop. Don't worry about me, you do you. I will support you and honey, I really like him. He's handsome and I think he will be good for you. He doesn't care what people think and I feel like he will show you things," she says.

I snicker and smile, "Yeah, show me a lot."

"Okay, I'm open to this, but no details baby," she says throwing her head back and laughing.

"Oh my God, Ma! Stop!" I say laughing.

"Just be happy. I want you to be happy. I see that with him," she shrugs her shoulders and smiles. "I like him, what can I say?"

"I like him too, momma. I really like him too."

∞ ∞ ∞

I leave my mom's house and head back to my townhouse. I'm about to pull into my driveway when my phone starts ringing. I glance down and smile.

"Hey, handsome," I say answering the phone.

"The eagle has landed," Patrick says on the other end.

"That was fast. Good flight?" I ask.

"Yeah, the other luxury of a private plane, none of the commercial airline bullshit. I don't want to go back to the real world tomorrow. Ugh," he says.

"Yeah, I have a new patient tomorrow. I'm looking forward to it, actually. I think after being with you and opening up myself to the possibility of having an actual relationship and being my true self, I really can help more. I always felt sort of guilty, like I was living a lie and then trying to help others cope with their anxieties of living an alternate lifestyle, I was being a hypocrite.

"That's wonderful, William. It really is. I love that you are feeling better about all this. I know this isn't easy for you. I really want all of this to be perfect for you." He says.

"Patrick, it will never be perfect. Life seldom is, but I know that having you will definitely make it better and pretty damn near close to perfect," I say smiling.

"Well aren't you the sweetest. I know this isn't the ideal situation. We are a thousand miles apart. But in my heart, I'm right there with you, you know. I've never felt so close to someone so far away," he sighs into the phone. "I miss you."

"I miss you too. When are you going to be coming out here again? After the honeymoon, maybe?" I say wishing it to be true.

"Unfortunately, I don't support much of that end of the business. That doesn't mean I can't come out. I can do most of my stuff remotely, just not all. I'm dealing with an issue right now with one of the construction sites. It's unconventional, but it's the way Logan works. He looks to find ways to solve problems by getting support from the neighbors of the city he is trying to improve. There have been a few issues with his latest improvement project, and he's formed an alliance with a motorcycle club that has rule over the territory. They have been trying to clean up the towns around them too and with a billion dollar investor, they are more than happy to help. As long as he turns his back on anything they may be doing. He struggles with it, but he knows that in the end, there will be a cleaner environment, with jobs and a city that will grow," he says.

"So, this motorcycle club may be doing illegal things, but because they are cleaning up the city, so to speak, it's okay? That seems kind of fucked up," I say.

"For the greater good. You may not agree, I don't know if I even do, but the improvement in safety in these neighborhoods have improved, there are new jobs and a general feeling of wellness. You would think the club would generate a different kind of feel, but it doesn't. These people know what it used to be like and they actually welcome them. They are treated like Gods there. It's pretty surreal. Just imagine not being able to sit out on your porch and enjoy the evening, or a bonfire like we did out there. They never were able to do that in fear of a drive-by shooting. Now, they sit out and actually have cookouts with neighbors. People are moving in, businesses are moving in and the towns that Logan invests in are thriving," he says.

"Well, it seems to be working. I can't blame his logic. You sometimes have to fight fire with fire. That still doesn't tell me when I'm going to see you again. Sorry, I don't mean to make this all about me," I sigh.

"Hey now, it's okay. I want to see you just as bad. Do you think you can get any time off? Come spend some time out here with me? I would love it." He says in a sing song voice.

"I never take vacation time, so I have a lot built up. I just don't know how soon I can get off. I would need to rearrange all my appointments. Let me try to figure it out tomorrow. I'll let you know as soon as I can," I respond.

"Sounds like a plan. Hey, I really do miss you."

"I miss you too. I'll try to work it out. Sweet dreams, sweet prince," I say yawning.

"Sweet dreams. I wish I was there to tuck you in and give you a hug," his voice goes soft. "I wish I could feel your lips and your body against mine. I would love to feel your cock get hard against my back, knowing it could enter me at any time. To have you take me and make me yours. I just want to be yours," he whispers.

"You are mine. And I am yours. I've never felt so connected before. We will work this out. Good night, babe," I say yawning.

We hang up and I hold the phone to my chest. I think about the last time we were together and I grow hard. Taking myself in my hand, I stroke myself hard until I cum all over my stomach.

Chapter Nine

Patrick

I want to make sure that the distance doesn't sink us before we even get started. I think the distance is actually a good thing. Sex with William is off the charts, and I could really get lost and consumed with that. I want to make sure there is depth in this relationship. Not seeing him when I want is hard, but missing him makes me feel closer to him if that makes sense.

I call Mick and find out what favorite go to snack items that William likes. I had to laugh when I asked him using William and not Buddy. It took him a few minutes to realize who I was talking about.

"Dude, I've only ever known him as Buddy. You can't just go changing his name and think I'd know who ya'll was talking about," he says laughing.

"Well, who else would I be talking about?" I laugh.

“I don’t know, but shit, I need to get used to you calling him by his real name,” Mick says and then starts rattling off various things that he knows William likes.

I take my lunch break and run to the store. I find a basket and just start filling it with random snacks. From red licorice to beef jerky and other various fun items. I found some old school stuff like pop rocks and the lick a stick thing. I throw in a stuffed bear that has black-rimmed glasses and buy a gold bracelet that I wrap around the bear’s wrist. I put it all together and put it in a box and run to the local shipment store. I hesitate about where to send it, but because it’s in a box, I think it will be okay to send to his practice.

I send it overnight, so he’ll get it tomorrow. I’m excited to get his reaction and nervous at the same time.

We send each other text messages throughout the day. They are not much, but I think it’s about consistency. I make sure that I send something to him and never let more than three hours go by.

The time difference can suck. It’s late for him when I go to bed and too early for me when he goes to bed. We try to still video call each other whenever we can.

Seeing his face lights my soul on fire. The butterflies hit me full force. I love that feeling. I know it’s new and amazing, but I also feel like it's something so special. How do I make sure it lasts the test of time?

The night of him receiving my gift, I get a call that is pretty late for him. I smile as I see him with a red licorice stick hanging from his mouth.

"You tryin' to get me to gain weight or what? Holy shit, Patrick. Thank you," he says.

"Just a little something to put in your mouth, since I can't be there," I snicker.

William gives me a smile and scans the phone down so I see his hard cock in his hand as he slowly strokes. I see he's wearing the bracelet I bought him.

"Looks tasty," I say licking my lips. "You make me feel so sexy, so important and valued," I say as I set my phone on my nightstand and angling it so he can see my whole body. I slowly push my gym shorts down and free my already hard cock.

"You are sexy and fucking hot," he says setting his phone down so I also can see him.

I watch as he rolls his one hand down his shaft as he squeezed his balls in the other. My cock jumps when I hear his moan and my eyes quickly look up to see him sucking in his bottom lip.

"Fuck I wish I was there. I would suck that lip for you," I say as I mimic his movements, the timing of our hands stroking are completely in sync.

"I wish you were here too, but I'd have something else for you to suck," he growls, and he speeds up.

"I don't even need to watch you, even though it's so intoxicating, all I need is to listen to the noises you make, and I'm going to blow," I say trying to maintain control.

"Then come for me, Patrick," he says with such command that my eyes immediately open and lock with his. "That's it."

"Fuck!" I shout as I feel my orgasm travel through my whole body and out the tip of my cock.

"Yes!" he yells never taking his eyes off me. I can't hold his stare. I want to watch as he comes.

I glance down just in time to see his release. I see the streams of his cum as it hits his stomach. The way he taps his cock against his stomach is erotic and I can't stop coming. My toes curl as the last of my orgasm travels through me.

"Dude. That was so fucking hot," I say trying to catch my breath.

“That was hot, Patrick. I miss you,” he says picking up his phone and bringing it closer to his face.

“I miss that fucking face. You are so incredibly handsome. When can I get you to come out here?” I ask.

“I totally didn’t get a chance to look today. I was super busy. It may not be for a few weeks though. I can’t just bail on my patients, unfortunately,” he says with a sly grin.

“Wouldn’t want you to. We will work it out. Good night, Doc. I’ll text you tomorrow,” I say making a kissing noise.

“Until tomorrow,” he says making the kissing noise back.

We hang up and I roll to my side holding my phone against my chest. He makes me feel things I’ve never felt. I only pray we can get over this distance and one day be on the same side of the country, no matter where that may be.

Chapter Ten

Buddy

I really want to get him something now, but I don't want to do it just because he got me something. I really suck at being in a real relationship.

I have to laugh at how I'm struggling over the simplest of things I had a fake girlfriend for fuck's sake. Keyword: fake. I didn't have to get her gifts or make sure I checked in with her. This is unchartered territory for me.

The difference this time is I want to talk to him all the time. I want to reach out and check in with him. I see those stupid ads online and I think about Patrick.

I think about the time Patrick came out and dressed in country western attire from head to toe and reminded me of that dating site commercial. I laughed my ass off. The way he pulled off the flower girl slash ring bearer was epic.

I tried to think of getting him something funny. Like a Ghillie suit or something. I can see him running around trying to hide in the brush and jumping out to scare people. I start laughing at how much fun he would have with it.

I know he wants me to come out to see him and I may be able to in October, so I'm wondering if I can time it around Halloween. I have no idea what I would dress up as though. I keep thinking to dress up like a deer or bear, but that seems too basic.

I need to make sure I can get all my patients scheduled around that time before I even think about taking it off.

My first patient of the day is one that I work with every week. She's a sweet, but troubled teen that thinks nothing is ever her fault. Her parents are ready to give up and she's not listening to me either. I don't want to roll my eyes, but shit it can be hard.

I want to stand up and just yell at her, but how professional would that be? Instead, I take a different approach and ask her if she can change how she reacts to people that obviously make her do the things she does. Instead of punching someone for doing something that offends her or pisses her off, what else could she do?

By the end of the session, I feel like we may have made a break through. I told her that she is stronger by walking away. She used a few choice words, but I think she basically realized that by giving into other people's actions, made her the weak one. I asked her who was at fault if others believed she was in the wrong. She immediately said it was theirs, so I said, well then who's fault is it when she thought they were in the wrong. She took a second and crossed her arms.

"Mine," she says with a smirk. "I see what you did there, but I get it. I'm in control of my actions."

"Exactly. You are the strong one. By giving into reacting to the way they treat you, you are giving them power. Get that power back. Smile and move along," I say.

She was smiling when she left. I think it was the first time I saw her smile.

It's times like this that I love what I do. Teens today have so much coming at them with the pressure of the normal things and the over stimuli of the constant online presence. I try to keep that in mind when I'm dealing with the younger patients.

I don't have another appointment for an hour, so I decide to try to work out my schedule for time off. I call the office secretary in and we sit down to find a good date.

After shuffling around a few, I get a full open week. I can't remember the last time I was able to take more than one day off. I wish I could do it as a surprise, but maybe I can. It's not like I can't afford to get my own ticket and just show up. I don't like the idea of being catered to anyways.

I decide to go online and purchase my own tickets. This should be interesting. I know he wants to take care of things, but I've never been one to let that happen. I want to take care of him.

I'm not sure how to get away with this though. I don't want to tell him to take vacation time, because he'll know. I'll have to get with Logan when he gets back from the honeymoon and see if he has any suggestions. He is Patrick's boss, after all.

My next patient is waiting so I shuffle my thoughts to the back of my mind and prepare. He's a ten year old that has high anxiety and I fear he is being bullied. The younger patients are the hardest. Getting them to talk is even harder. However, if you find the magic potion to get them to open up, it's gold. It takes me about fifteen minutes to hit that golden spot. By simply relating to him as also being bullied, he starts to spill. It's heartbreaking, but after our session, he hugs me. I've hit two for two today, but I'm mentally exhausted. Thankfully, that was my last one for the day and I head home.

Once I enter my house, I crash on the couch. I'm surprised that I've slept for three hours. Looks like tomorrow will be fun since I won't be able to get to sleep any time soon.

I also missed a few texts from Patrick. The last one seems like he's worried. I send back a reply to let him know that I had fallen asleep but don't get an immediate reply as I usually do. Self-doubt enters my head. I send off another text letting him know I'm awake but still don't get a reply.

Why do I even do this? I'm not ready for this and fuck if I know how to do the long distance. He could be fucking anyone right now and I would never know. I'm not a jealous person, but that ugly green monster starts to put all kinds of things in my head. I toss my phone to the end of the couch and get up to get something to eat.

I hear it buzzing a short time later, but I'm in the wrong mind set to even check it. I should just put this thing to rest and stop. He's not going to move here and I don't want to move there so why am I even trying to get invested in a relationship that won't last? Fuck.

The buzzing continues until I can't stand it any longer. I sit down on the couch and grab my phone. Taking a deep breath, I flip it over to several missed calls and texts.

I only read the last one. "If you think I'm going away any time soon, you are wrong. Go back and read my texts and listen to my voicemails. I know this is hard, but I told you that I was all in, and that will not change. Even if you think you want it to. Doc, I'm yours. So get out of that head of yours. Call me when you come back to reality. Because reality is us."

I listen through the voicemails and hear that he had to go to a clubhouse and give up his phone once he entered. He tells me that they are the motorcycle club that is patrolling the area of Logan's latest projects making sure nothing happens with the local gangs. They are trying to run the gangs out and it's been a task.

There is about a two hour delay between messages. I start laughing as he dramatically replays his time inside.

"Babe, holy shit. The guy who runs the club, who they call the President and is named "Rev". He was huge! He shook my hand and I thought all my bones were breaking. It's unreal. They are all in leather and look like they could snap me in half with their pinkies. I was so scared. But they were actually nice. As far as bikers go. Here I am, a queen, in a biker clubhouse trying to act tough when I was actually shitting my pants. And then, this beautiful woman comes out of nowhere and sits on this Rev guy's lap. His demeanor totally changes before my eyes. Like he bows down to her. It was unreal. If I wouldn't have seen it with my own eyes. Babe, this was an experience I don't know if I could do again. Wow, I'm still shaking." He says.

I get a few more texts and voicemails all of which ask why I'm not answering and not to be mad. I have to laugh at the last voicemail that says, "Don't be jealous. I'm not falling for the president or any of these biker dudes. Please answer me. I know you have your doubts about us. Don't let one instance of me not being available make you take a turn to the dark side. I'm still here. I'll always be here."

I hold my phone and decide to just call him. He answers immediately, "Are you out of your head?"

"Yeah, I am. Sorry" I say.

"This is going to happen. We are far away from each other and we are still building our relationship. But trust needs to be a foundation. I will never do anything to betray you. I told you, I'm all in. I can't expect you to trust me at first, I know this. I also know this is new for you. Just promise me you will hear me out. That you won't jump to your own conclusions without talking to me first. Please."

"I'll try. I can't make you any promises, because as you said, this is all new to me. I never thought I was a jealous person, and I do trust you. It's not about trust or about you, it's me overcoming my own doubt. I'll get there. Please be patient."

"Just talk to me. Please don't disappear, hide or ignore me. I care about you, Doc. I don't like being worried and dude, you had me worried," he says.

"Yeah, well, I'll try. Just call me out on my shit. I know I am the more dominant one, but I need you to step up every once in a while." I say.

"You're scared. I get that. It's not that hard, really. Trust me. Don't try too hard or you will feel like you are failing. Just let it flow naturally. Let me be your guide to love," he says in a deep comedic voice that has me laughing.

"My love guru," I say chuckling.

"Damn right," he says, "Namaste, Doc."

Chapter Eleven

Patrick

It scares me that this even happened. I just wish I could pack up my shit and move out there. I don't want to move though, I would rather have him out here. That's a whole other issue to overcome. I know he loves his mountains. All of them there do, that's why everyone else has moved.

I just know that I love where I'm at. I love the openness and acceptance. I love the noise and hustle of the city. I also love Logan's house. I've been spending a lot of time there since he's left. At first it was because I thought it was so I could feel close to him. Now, it's more because it reminds me of the mountains. It's so much quieter and more secluded.

I want to ask Logan if I can rent from him, but I know I can't afford the mortgage on his place. I don't want a handout, but it's becoming to feel like home to me and I don't know how I'll feel if I have to give it up.

Today was interesting. I told Logan that I would deal with communication with the motorcycle club that has been helping with weeding out the gangs in the area of the improvement properties. I had to do a check in, and it meant that I had to go to their clubhouse.

I've seen the TV shows about the MCs and it's not always an actual depiction of reality, but this was pretty close.

I was met immediately at the gate by a mean looking guy in a leather vest. I saw "prospect" on the chest and for some reason, I smiled. It was like the shows in real life.

He asked me my business, and I said I was Logan Cartwright's assistant here to check in with Rev. He makes a call and a few minutes later, waves me inside, closing the gate behind me.

Unlike a bar establishment, it's a huge warehouse. When I walk through the steel door, I suck in a breath. It's so different on the inside. It's clean and almost opulent as far as warehouses go.

There is artwork on the walls and big oversized couches placed in sections. There's a full bar with lights hanging around that makes you think you have entered an elite nightclub. It's weird.

I'm asked to immediately drop my cell phone into a basket by the door. I look around and expect to see waiters with bow ties, but all I see is men in leather vests and tattoos. Beards and hair at different lengths. It's a walking oxymoron. The women aren't trashy looking, they are in designer dresses and heels with red soles. These are not the typical half-dressed women you would expect.

There are some questionable items though. I see what looks like a St. Andrew's cross set back in one corner on a stage. There's a wall of what I would imagine to see in that red room in that BDSM bestseller.

Holy shit. What kind of club is this?

The prospect who said his name was Crumbs, walks me over to one of the sectionals. There's a man sitting with his one leg propped up on the other and leaning back in a relaxed state. I watch his foot gingerly bounce up and down as he smiles at me as I walk forward.

"Patrick?" he asks and motions for me to sit down.

"Yeah...umm...Rev, I suppose?" I say taking a wide berth to sit on the furthest spot away from him.

"Welcome to the Lion's Den," he motions his hand around. There's a slight accent that I can't quite detect where it's from.

"This place is pretty awesome. Sorry, but it wasn't at all what I had expected," I say looking around.

“Well, we are not a typical club. I like tidy and clean and think if you want respect, you need to respect everything. Even the space you dwell in. We may not respect the “man”, but we respect ourselves. Those who don’t, are not welcome. You look like someone that respects themselves and others. That’s the thing that I like about Logan. He’s a good man, who shows and expects respect. I’ve been happy to help him clean up things,” he says as a woman dressed in complete stunning leather approaches.

She’s amazingly beautiful. For a woman, that is. Long dark hair that shines under the lights. She’s wearing four inch spiked heels that she moves in with ease.

She takes a seat right on his lap and kisses him like I’m not even there.

“Love, this is Patrick. He’s Logan’s assistant and just checking on things.” He says. He tucks his head and I find that a bit weird.

“Hello, Patrick. I’m this guy’s Ol’ Lady,” she gives a half chuckle, “My name is Gabriella. It’s nice to meet you.”

“My queen, not my old lady. Always my queen,” he says as they dive into each other again.

I clear my throat and try not to feel like I'm imposing. I can't seem to take my eyes off of them.

"Nice to meet you, too. I just wanted to stop by since Logan is on his honeymoon and check in to see if there are any new concerns since the last incident?" I end in a question.

"Nope. I think we ran the little assholes out. I won't go into details, but we sent a decent message. It's what we do, and we have never been unsuccessful. I don't think you will have any more issues, but we will keep a presence to make sure. You need a drink or anything? Crumbs, get Patrick a drink," he yells.

I don't know if I should contradict the president, but I really don't want a drink. "Hey, Crumbs, I'm good dude. Thank you. If that's okay."

"Submissive. I see it, but I like that you can take control when you need to. Respect, man," Rev says motioning Crumbs off.

"How? Okay, I think I'm going to get going. I'll let Logan know you have things under control. If you need anything, let me know. I really do love this place. I've never been on a bike, but do you let outsiders come in to just hang out? I wouldn't mind coming, not on business," I say as I stand.

"I apologize for not standing, but I have this luscious angel on my lap that kind of controls me," he says as Gabriella smiles and snuggles into him.

"It's all good. Gabriella, Rev, so nice to meet you and I hope to see you both again." I say truly meaning it.

"Same here. You are always welcome. If you ever want to tap into that submissive side, just let me know. I may have someone in mind for you," Gabriella says and surprises me that it was her and not Rev.

"I have a man. He's all the dominant I want in my life right now," I say smiling.

"Well, if you ever want to experience him dominating you in a private, but public environment, let me know," she says returning my smile.

Again, as I will repeat over and over again, holy shit. What just happened? I head out and grab my phone and see that I've gotten a few text and voicemails from William.

I know right away that he is questioning things. I can see desperation in the messages. Dammit. I need to fix it and get the fuck home.

This has been a very strange experience and now I have to make sure my boyfriend is okay. He's my top priority and since I couldn't have my phone, I feel like I already let him down.

After our conversation, I feel better. I still didn't tell him all that happened at the clubhouse. I need to tell him about this tomorrow. My mind is still spinning. What kind of MC is this? If I said I wasn't intrigued, I would be lying.

Chapter Twelve

Buddy

There's nothing better than knowing you are thought about. It's surreal that I get little texts throughout the day. It makes me feel something I never thought I would ever feel. Loved.

"Hey, handsome," Patrick says as I answer the phone.

"Hey, sexy," I say back with a smile in my voice.

"So, I didn't get to tell you all about my experience last night at the club. Oh my God, Doc. This place was not what you would have expected of a one percent motorcycle club. I mean it was clean. Here is this dirty looking warehouse on the outside, but when you get inside, it was like an upscale club. Even the girls were classy looking. However. I'm not even sure how to even say this," he says chuckling.

"Well, you have my full attention now. What else?" I say really intrigued.

"Weelll," he says overdrawing it. "There was a St. Andrew's cross in the back corner and questionable items hanging from the wall," he says with a slight shrill.

"Like what?" I say lowering my voice and starting to grow hard.

"Doc. Fuck, when you lower your voice like that, shit," he says. "There were whips and things? You know," he says almost sounding embarrassed.

"Are you embarrassed, Patrick?" I ask with a little more force.

"Yes, a little. I've never done any of that stuff, but she knew somehow," Patrick says almost ending in a whisper.

"Who? Knew what?" I ask trying to get him to let his guard down.

"Gabriella. She was the president's, wife, girlfriend, old lady, I don't know, but she called me a submissive," he says mumbling the last word.

"How did you feel about that?" I ask.

"Are you doing the Doc thing or the dominate thing here? I'm a little confused," he says.

“Just answer me.” I state firmly, needing to know.

“So, you are doing the dominate thing, okay,” he says. “I was nervous, I won’t lie. I was also wondering what I would be like. Mainly, wondering if anyone would even want to see a man being dominated by another man. I also wondered what all those things on the wall were. I’ve never explored the world of BDSM. I don’t think I could handle pain, but I’ve done some research and well, I don’t really know what to think, honestly. This may sound weird, but I’m traditional. Even though I love men, I still look at is as wanting a traditional relationship. I’m not sure of the kink part. That doesn’t mean that I’m not open to exploring. I know when you take control, I’m all in. I won’t deny that I submit to you. I won’t deny that you have the control. I’m willing to give it to you.”

“Damn, Patrick. I never thought of myself as a dominant, but yeah, I guess I am. I would never push you to do anything that you didn’t want. I love that when I tell you to do something, you do it. I never thought that I was that kind of person. I tend to be more reserved, but you bring something out of me that I’ve never felt before. I want to be your partner, but I also want to control you, but only in the bedroom. Otherwise, we are equal,” I say thinking I’m screwing this all up.

"I give you permission to control me in the bedroom, Sir," he says and hesitates before letting out a snort. "Sorry. Can we just let it happen without trying to define it?"

"Of course. I love that we were able to have this conversation, to begin with. You said that communication was key and I think this was important. I don't ever want you to think that anything was off topic. I want full disclosure. Always," I say.

"Always," he says. "You control the bedroom and I'll try to control everything outside of it."

"That's a lot to control to be responsible for, Patrick. I don't want you to think that I can't take control outside of the bed and I want you to have some control inside the bedroom too," I say trying to make sure he understands I'm not a control freak.

"Learn as we go, agree?" Patrick says.

"I'll agree to that. I have a lot to learn," I say taking a deep breath.

"You know, we just have to get you there." Patrick laughs. "I like where this is going. I've never been able to open up completely with anyone, but I find myself doing so with you."

"Well, looks like we are learning together. As it should be," I say. "I can't wait to see you."

∞ ∞ ∞

It's getting close to the time for my trip to LA. I am so nervous about going out there.

Logan and Presley Ann are back from their honeymoon and agreed to meet me for dinner. I'm hoping to get information and possible help to surprise Patrick.

Logan asks why I didn't ask him to fly me out, and I immediately waved him off. "I don't want to sound ungrateful, Logan. But, I don't want to take advantage of you. I will, however; take advantage of any car service you may have to get me to Patrick."

"What time does your flight land? I can get you car service and depending on when will depend on where I send you. I got you either way," he says pulling out his phone.

"I appreciate it. My flight lands around four Pacific Time," I say looking at my itinerary info.

"Okay, so I'll make sure he's still in the office. He usually is anyways, but I'll make sure of it. I'll even have the chauffer stop by a local cupcake shop. You will get very far showing up with cupcakes, just saying. The boy may be fit and thin, but he loves his sweets," Logan says laughing.

"Shit, there is so much I need to learn about him," I say adjusting my glasses.

"Buddy. I've known Patrick for a few years now. We've been side by side on a daily basis. You guys have just come together, really quick, but I feel you have something to last a lifetime. I don't want to say I'm an expert, but when I met this girl right here, I knew," he says taking Presley Ann's hand and giving it a kiss.

"There was something in my gut the first time I met him. I keep doubting myself though. This is my first real true relationship," I say.

"That alone seems like a challenge from the start, but you can't focus on that. If you do, you will self-destruct. You need to just focus on the now and on the two of you. Nothing else. You will have a lot of challenges. Even more so because of this being a gay relationship. I don't envy you, but I pray that the outside world doesn't affect you. Shut it out, if you can. We're here for you. Don't forget the circle and the people in your corner. We love both of you and will be cheering from the sidelines," Presley Ann says reaching out for my hand.

"I just want this to work. I think I'm in love with him, guys. I'm so scared of going to LA and getting overwhelmed and bailing," I say squeezing her hand.

"Buddy, I get it. I was there and Lord Almighty, I was way out of my comfort zone. If you remember, I freaked out and came home. Those shit people are the devil. Yet, look at how it turned out. I have the man of my dreams. Promise to call me if you get overwhelmed. I'll get it better than anyone else," Presley Ann says.

"I promise. Thank you, Logan, for helping me with this. It means a lot."

"Dude, Patrick is like my brother. I'm so happy for him and you. I'll always be here for you two. If my angel doesn't help you, I'm a phone call away. I know Patrick better than anyone. I got your back."

"I appreciate you two so much. I'm so blessed. I won't forget it. Wish me luck, I think I'll need it," I sigh.

"You and Patrick have us. Love you," Presley Ann says.

Chapter Thirteen

Patrick

I haven't heard from William since this morning. My texts were not returned at lunch. I'm in my head as I get a call from the front desk downstairs.

"You have a delivery," the front desk clerk says.

"Oh yay! Send it up!" I say wondering what it is.

I've been sitting in Logan's office. Sue me. He's not here and there is so much more room. Plus, it makes me feel more important. Logan doesn't care. I have the office door open and hear the ding of the elevator, so I jump out and jog to the hallway.

When the doors open, I just about squeal. I see the fedora first and then my William's face as he steps off the elevator with a box in his hands.

I see heads pop up over cubicles and try to contain myself. I don't want him to feel uncomfortable, but I just want to run to him and pull him into my arms.

His smile is amazing. I stop dead in my tracks and just take him in, "You're here. How are you here? Wait, shit is that why Logan really had me clear my calendar for a few days this week? He said he thought that he may need me to go deal with shit with Rev and that it may take longer than we'd like. I'll have to thank him," I say grabbing his hand and pulling him into Logan's office and shutting the door.

"I'm here bearing cupcakes. Logan advised me to," he says once we are alone.

"Fuck the cupcakes. You are so much sweeter," I say setting the box on the table beside the door. I grab his face and press my lips against his, "God I missed you."

"I've missed you too," he says between kisses. "God, how I have missed you."

"You are here. Shit. Let me make a few calls and wrap this up. I'm off the rest of the time you are here," I say rushing over to the desk.

I glance up to see him slowly pulling the cupcake liner down and looking seductively over his glasses. It's cute and sexy. "Bring me one, hot stuff."

About an hour later and with all the cupcakes gone, I lick my fingers and shut down my laptop. "You have me for the next few days. I should have saved some of the icing for later."

"I'm sure we will be able to come up with an alternative," he says smiling.

"So, I don't remember seeing a manifest for the plane. I did see service for the car, but didn't really think about it. How did you get here?" I ask standing and unbuttoning the cuffs of my shirt and rolling them up.

"Logan gave me a hard time, but I went commercial. I didn't want to seem like I was taking advantage of him. Besides, I can pay my own way. I haven't taken a real vacation since I've started at the practice," he says shrugging his shoulders.

"I get it. I say it's perks of the job, but I can understand how you would feel about it," I say tossing the empty cupcake box into the trash. "Hungry? Let's go grab dinner."

"I'm starving," he says following me out of the office to the elevator.

I let him catch up and go to wrap my arm around his waist. He jerks quickly away and looks around with a slight look of panic.

"I'm sorry. I...I keep forgetting," I say tucking my hands into my pockets.

"No, I'm sorry. I didn't mean to react that harshly," he says leaning into me and giving me a soft smile.

On the elevator ride down, I try to reassure him more. "Remember, no one knows you here. This is your opportunity to let go and enjoy things about being a gay man without judgment. Well, we may still get looks don't get me wrong. It's just accepted here more than other places. However, I will remember to keep your feelings in mind and go at your pace."

"I want to let go. It's not going to happen immediately. I appreciate your patience," he says giving me a quick kiss on the cheek before the doors open.

I walk everywhere. I actually live just a few blocks down from the office. It suddenly hits me that William doesn't have any bags.

"Where is your luggage, Doc?" I stop and ask.

"Oh, the driver said he would drop it off at your apartment. I figured that was okay," he says.

"Oh, that's perfect. Rudy the doorman will hold it for you until we get there. Do you want to head over there and change or anything, or just go and grab something to eat now?" I ask.

"Do I look okay? I can change if you think I should," he says running his hands down the front of his buttoned down shirt.

"You look sexy as fuck. I didn't want to assume anything and want to make sure you are good," I say smiling as I take him in. I'm so excited that he's actually standing on the sidewalk with me here.

"I'm good. Let's eat," he says cocking his head. "You have the most amazing smile."

"I'm just so excited that you are here. I feel like I'm in the best dream ever," smiling even bigger. "Like you said, let's eat. Follow me."

We walk around the corner and down the street a little. There's a little Italian bistro that has a cute outdoor patio. I love it because you can people watch and sometimes run into famous people.

The hostess greets me personally and grabs two menus. She takes me to my favorite table outside. When she hands William a menu, he immediately says, “Thank ya, ma’am.”

“Oh my God. I love your accent. Where are you from?” she ask.

“Tennessee, ma’am,” he replies.

Giggling, she says “A southern gentleman. It’s a pleasure to meet you. Any friend of Patrick’s is a friend of mine. Lola will be over to get your order and take care of you this evening.”

She waves goodbye as she goes back out to the front of the restaurant and we fall into an easy conversation.

He suddenly stops and his eyes go wide. “Is that...? Oh my God.”

I look up and see a famous face. I’m excited that he’s here with his husband. I was hoping that William would see firsthand how open it is here. I don’t want to push him. I just want him to be comfortable and let go like I had mentioned in the elevator.

"This is unreal. I don't want to keep staring, but they are just holding hands so naturally," he says almost in awe.

"I'm glad you get to witness it. I told you. It's not uncommon and not unnatural here," I smile as I take in his face.

He looks around quickly and then reaches over and grabs my hand. It's a simple gesture, but my heart almost wants to burst out of my chest. I feel like I want to cry. I squeeze his hand and keep my head down looking at my menu as I try to reel in my emotions.

Clearing my throat, I tell him about the different things on the menu and point out my favorites.

We both agree to get the antipasto salad and share two different entrees. I got the veal parmesan and William got the chicken alfredo.

Our meals come and William gets to see a few more famous faces and a few more open couples of all sorts. This is the reason I love living here. Nothing is shocking to see. In fact, being an openly gay man can be looked at as just as traditional as a relationship between a man and a woman. There are open polyamorous of all different sorts, of which seem still more shocking to witness. Just as the thought entered my mind, four people walk in all arm in arm. Two men and two woman exchanging kisses between each other.

I glance over at William and see him quickly glance back and forth between them and me with his eyebrow raised.

"Welcome to my neck of the woods," I say laughing and continuing to eat like it was normal.

Feeling like I'm going to explode, I lean back in my chair. I place my arm around the back of William's chair and rub my belly with the other.

I'm surprised when he leans back and slightly into me, "That was so good, and I'm stuffed. Probably shouldn't have eaten those cupcakes."

"You are amazing and eating dessert before dinner is always a good thing. We can go to the gym tomorrow to work this all off. Wait until you see the people that work out at my gym. You think you got some sights this evening?" I say moving my arm slowly around his shoulders. Cautiously gauging his response, I'm pleased when he settles in against me and lets out a sigh.

"I can get used to this."

"Me too, Doc. Me too,"

Chapter Fourteen

Buddy

I'm sitting here arm and arm with another man. Out in the open on the patio of a restaurant as people walk by. No one cares. No one even glances our way.

I feel alive for the first time. I realize that I haven't truly been living. I've been existing and hiding. I've been afraid to live because I was afraid of the hurtful things that would happen to my ma.

She always said she was strong enough to handle it. If I'm being honest, the truth is, I wasn't. I was more afraid of how people would treat me. I was selfish.

I'm still scared, but somehow, I think maybe I'm ready to be free.

On our way back to Patrick's apartment, I wrap my arm around Patrick's waist. He leans into me with a smile.

"Baby steps," Patrick says.

“Yeah, don’t expect me to jump in with both feet just yet,” I say.

We get to his apartment and get my luggage from behind the front desk. We head up and when we step inside, I instantly feel Patrick in the room. He’s beside me, physically yes, but it’s more, he’s surrounds me, consumes me. He make me feel like I’m home.

His place is comfortable. It’s clean but welcoming. There’s a pop of color everywhere. He has a black leather sectional in the middle of the room, but there are throw pillows of mosaic colors thrown about.

They match the colors in the rug on the floor. I laugh when I see a stuffed unicorn tucked into the corner of the couch.

“My bedroom is this way,” Patrick says setting his keys in a bowl by the door.

I follow him down the hallway and glance back and forth at a collage of photos on the wall. I see a few familiar faces of him and Logan. Him and Marissa. What I assume is his family. I stop in my tracks when I see a photo of us sitting by the campfire at one of our gatherings in Tennessee.

"How did you get this?" I ask as I look at the picture and see that we are not sitting next to each other, but we are clearly looking and smiling at one another.

"Well, I kind of stole that one from Missy Jo. But I have to be honest. When I first saw it, I just saw a group of great people that I had met and had gotten close to. I was so consumed by Logan, that I didn't see it for what it truly was," he says.

"And what do you see now?" I ask.

"My soul connecting. I see you and me connecting," he says leaning against the wall staring at it with a smile.

I look back at it and I see it too. Two people looking at each other with a visible connection.

I let go of my luggage and step forward pushing myself against him. "I see us."

Taking his face into my hands, I look deep into his eyes and see his pupils start to dilate. "I need to bury myself so far inside you that neither of us knows where my body ends and your body begins."

"Fuck," he exclaims and pulls me closer.

Our lips meet in a frenzy as we grab and tug each other's clothes off. Both naked, Patrick pulls me into his bedroom and I find myself pushed back, falling onto his bed. Patrick falls to his knees at the foot of the bed and spreads my legs. He pulls me towards the edge of the bed and moves between my legs.

Wrapping his hand around my cock he gives it a stroke and sends pleasure through my body. I lift up onto my elbows as I watch him continue to stroke me, slowly rolling his tongue around my tip.

"Fuck that feels good," I moan, trying not to throw my head back.

The bedroom is dark, but there's light coming in from the hallway so I can still see what he is doing. His tongue continues to roll around and I feel as he slowly takes me into his mouth.

He looks up at me as he takes me deeper and I can't help but run my fingers through his hair and push him down further.

I can no longer hold eye contact as the pressure of my orgasm starts to hit. "Fuck, Patrick. I'm going to cum."

I feel him massage my balls as he presses a finger into my ass and I'm done.

I thrust up as he opens his throat and takes me deep. Feeling his finger in my ass as his throat squeezes around my cock, I cum hard., it was too much, I couldn't hold back my orgasm.

I feel Patrick crawl onto the bed and I find myself being pulled up as Patrick wraps me in his arms. I feel his hard cock against my back.

"I want you to take me," I say.

"What do you mean?" Patrick asks.

"I want you to be my first. I want you to make love to me, Patrick," I say rubbing his arms.

"You've never..."

"No, and I want it to be you, please," I say looking back at him.

"No fucking pressure here. Okay. I can do this," he says rolling over and pulling out a condom from his nightstand.

I sit up and push him down on the bed. Leaning over I stroke him and take him into my mouth. I'm just getting into in when he grunts and pulls me up, kissing me.

He rolls us over and looks into my eyes and sighs. "You are perfect. I'm falling for you, Doc."

"Make me yours," I say smiling.

Raising up he rolls on the condom and pulls out some lubricant. Squeezing some onto him and into his hand, I feel as he slowly rolls his finger around my ass and pushes it inside. It feels so good, I feel myself growing hard again.

I spread my legs wide as he slides his chest up mine and again looks right into my eyes. "Ready?"

I nod and take a deep breath. "I've never been more ready."

I feel the pressure as he slowly pushes forward. There's a slight pain at first, but then there is a feeling of complete euphoria.

"Fuck this is incredible," I say trying not to yell.

Patrick pushes forward and captures my lips in his. I feel him everywhere. His sweat mixes with mine as his thrusts increase. Our tongues roll around each other's while our hands explore each other.

I grab my knees and draw them up into my armpits and the pleasure increases. "Fuck, Patrick. Fuck me!" I yell out.

I never imagined it could be this good. I know I enjoy being on the other end, but receiving never seemed to interest me. I always hoped I brought pleasure and certainly hoped that I did with Patrick, but now I know. I know the pleasure that he felt and I'm going to cum.

"I'm going to cum, Patrick," I growl.

"Me too. Fuck, William," he grunts as he continues to thrust in and out.

I look into his eyes as I take his lips and say, "I love you, Patrick."

"Fuck! I love you too," he says as he grinds deep inside of me and I can feel him swell and pulse.

My orgasm hits at the same time and I empty onto my stomach as he grinds and spreads my cum between us.

Chapter Fifteen

Patrick

I forgot to turn off my daily alarm, so my phone goes beeping from out in the hallway. That's where I dropped my pants last night.

"Turn it off. For the love of baby Jesus, my body still has not adjusted to the time difference. Fuck!" William groans and buries his head under the covers and pillows.

I roll out of bed, pick up my pants from the hallway floor, digging my phone out and stop the alarm. I drop my pants back down to the floor and go to the bathroom. After I finish my morning routine, I slip out quietly and put on a pair of basketball shorts.

I start a pot of coffee. I want to cook him breakfast, but I know how early it is and how jet lagged he must still be. I decide to let him sleep and drink a cup of coffee while I go through some emails. May as well get some work done.

I smile as I think about last night. He let me take him and it was incredible. When he told me he loved me, I had that heart burst feeling again. He's here and in my bed and I don't want him to ever leave. I can't think about that now. He's going to be here for the next few days and I want to enjoy the time we have together.

I hear movement in the bedroom and glance at my watch. I've been at my emails for almost two hours. Damn, I wanted to make him breakfast in bed.

I jump up and quickly pour him a mug of coffee as he comes into the kitchen. "Sorry about this morning. I was going to let you sleep longer."

"It's okay. I get up pretty early when I'm working. Coffee...mmm...thank you. I slept great but..." he says making a face.

"What's wrong?" I ask stepping forward and cupping his chin.

He looks up at me and lets out a nervous chuckle and then looks away. "I'm. Well. Sore."

"Oh...Ohhhhh. I totally didn't think. I'm so sorry. Will you let me help with that?" I ask.

He nods his head but looks uncomfortable. "I'm not good with letting someone take care of me. Definitely not comfortable with my personal space like that. I know. It sounds weird. I'm a dominate for a reason. I like to have control and I'm not really good at giving it up."

"You gave it up last night," I joke as I give his chin a teasing nibble.

"I really loved it too. It's just out of character for me. You are lucky I love you," he says grabbing my chin and pressing his lips against mine. I feel his tongue come out and tease my bottom lip and run across it.

"I've never told anyone outside of friends and family that I loved them. I love you, William. So very much. You make my heart soar every time you give me a little piece of yourself. A piece that I think no one else has ever had of you. I treasure those moments. Let me take care of you. I want to be able to do that for you and for you to allow me. Please?" I ask.

"Well at this point, I need the relief. I'm...sore...but itchy," he says letting out a sigh.

"Oh, that's the worse. We need to take care of it before you get the dreading hems," I say grabbing his hand and pulling him to the master bathroom.

"I'm scared that I know what you are referring to and no I don't want those. Please, I'll do anything not to get the hems," he says actually starting to laugh.

"Awww, I'll take care of you, Doc," I say grabbing salve from my medicine cabinet. "The question is, do you want me to apply this, which will probably mean you will need to take a 'frisk me' stance, but I'll be able to make sure it gets applied properly."

William shrugs his shoulders and whips down his boxers. Bending at the waist, he places his hands on the sink counter and spreads his legs. "At your mercy."

I stop and look at him standing there. Running my eyes down from the top of his head to his bare feet. His body is so sexy. My hard-on is almost uncontrollable and with no underwear on, my erection is sticking straight out in my shorts.

"I see his eyes flare in the mirror as they glance down at my crotch and back up to my eyes. His mouth forms a smirk and he wiggles his ass back and forth.

"I'll take care of you if you take care of this damn sore itch. Please," he almost begs.

I dab my fingers into the tub of salve and rub them together with my thumb to warm it up. I use my other hand to spread his cheeks apart and lean down. I gently use two fingers to rub the salve around and make sure I push the salve into the opening just slightly and quickly.

"Oh yeah, that feels amazing. The itching and burning are going away, thank you," he sighs.

Before I can even set the jar of salve down, William spins around and wraps his arms around me. I'm then lifted and set on the sink where seconds earlier he was leaning. I don't know how he did it so fast and my head is still spinning.

I love how he takes my face into his hands and commands our kissing. He tilts my head the way he wants. Kissing him is always magical.

He runs his hands down and across my shoulders. Slowly down my arms and to the waistband of my shorts. I lift slightly to allow him to pull them over my ass and down to the floor. Our lips and tongues never stop exploring and devouring.

Running his hands back up my body and to my face, he pulls me back and looks deep into my eyes. "You have the most amazing eyes. Since I've known you, I've seen blue, green, gray and right now, they are the most brilliant of blues I've ever seen."

I smile and say, "Yours are badass. Like a tiger. I've never seen anything more mesmerizing."

He gives me a quick kiss to the lips and with a devilish smile, he kisses my chin and then my neck. He continues to kiss various parts of my chest and stomach. His hand wraps around my erection and pulls it away from my stomach. His lips kiss and suck all the way down to the bottom of my shaft and I jerk in his fist. He continues his kissing and sucking of my skin around until he reaches my balls and I can't help but throw my head back against the mirror.

I reach down and run my fingers through his thick hair. I love the feeling of his tongue as he presses under my balls before sucking one into his mouth.

He spends time on each one before running his lips and tongue around my shaft. His eyes flare when he looks up at me. They slowly close as he slowly moves up to my tip.

His hand is wrapped around my shaft and pushed down to the base. It makes my whole skin tight and the head of my cock seems more sensitive. So, when his tongue and lips tease me, my toes curl.

"Fuck, Doc. That feels so fucking good," I groan.

He hums before taking me fully in to where I can feel the back of his throat. I hold him by the back of his head and press his face against my stomach until I feel his nose flare.

I release him and he comes off me taking in a deep breath. There's saliva running down the corner of his mouth.

I'm not sure if the intensity of his stare is because he's pissed or turned on. He wipes his face with two fingers and shoves them into my mouth.

He continues to stroke me as I suck on his fingers. He takes in a deep breath, letting it out and diving back down on me. He takes me in and out. Once again opening his throat, I figure he was turned on, so I press him against me and hold him down until his nose flares again.

We continue these actions until I can't take it anymore. The last time I press him down on me, I explode down his throat. I feel his throat compress around my cock as he swallows.

I slap my hands down on the counter. William grabs my waist with both hands and pulls me harder towards him as he continues to try to breathe through his nose against me.

Coming up for air, he takes in one breath and presses his lips against mine. We continue to slowly kiss. I can taste the saltiness of my cum on him.

"That was sexy as fuck," he says folding me into his arms.

"I wasn't sure if I overstepped or not. I couldn't tell if you were pissed or not until you kept going," I say kissing his shoulder and rubbing his back.

"Definitely not pissed, babe," he says chuckling. "I wasn't expecting that from you, but it was such a turn on. Now feed me, I'm starving. Then I'll fuck you over the kitchen table."

"Well, that certainly sounds good to me," I say jumping off the sink and slipping my shorts on.

Chapter Sixteen

Buddy

I was embarrassed. I've never been bottom and even though I absolutely loved it, the morning after, not so much. I was sore and itching and overall uncomfortable.

Patrick took control and took care of me immediately, so I took care of him. I also let my submissive side out and let him take total control and it was sexy as fuck.

He cooked me an amazing breakfast and as promised, I fucked him on the table after we were done.

We then did the whole touristy things people do in LA. I was so excited. I had a few favorites. The tour where you sit on top of the bus driving around to visit houses of the stars was unreal. I couldn't believe the size of some of these homes. Some you could barely see, but you just knew it was opulent.

We then went and did the Hollywood Walk of Fame. It was kind of cheesy, but still fun. The best was when he took me to

Rodeo Drive. I was afraid to touch anything in the stores we walked into.

Patrick was the master though. He walked in like he owned the place and scored us free champagne at almost every store we walked into.

The best was when we walked into an amazing hat store. I love my fedoras, but I always wanted a page boy hat. It's old school and right up my alley.

The first hat I pick up isn't anything special but when I put it on my head, I'm in love. I take it off and look at the price tag and immediately put it back on the rack.

"That looked great on you. You should get it," Patrick says.

"Nah, it's okay but I'm not paying that much for a hat," I say.

"Well, I will. I want you to have it. Let me do this. Please," he says.

I pick it up and place it back on my head. "I really do like it. But holy shit, one hat should not cost two hundred and fifty bucks. I mean, I have money and all, but that's ridiculous."

"Let me get it for you. Again, please," he begs.

"Okay. Just this once. I really like it," I say turning from side to side checking out my profiles in the mirror.

"I love it. It's perfect for you," he says taking it from my head and walking to the counter to pay.

I struggle with him paying for this for me, but he wants to do it and he seems happy too. I don't want to take that away from him. It's just not something I normally am comfortable with.

After Patrick pays, he rips the tag off, grabs the fedora off my head and places it in the store bag. He then places my new hat on my head and gives me a quick kiss.

"Thank you. You didn't need to do that, you know," I say adjusting the hat.

"You bought me cupcakes and don't say anything about price. It's the gesture that counts. You like the hat. It looks amazing on you. I like cupcakes and you bought my favorite kind," he says smiling. "Never put a price tag on things. The value of the gesture means so much more."

"I like that and you are right. Too many people seem to put a price tag on things. You can't put a price tag on love," I say flicking my hat.

We leave the store hand in hand. I'm still amazed that we only get a few glances. The stigma is still there, but less here. I'm feeling so comfortable and so free to just be me. To show my love for this man in the open. I don't have to hide.

"So, I have something special planned. With Logan leaving, his house is up for grabs and he's willing to give it to me at a great price. I mean I am his assistant after all. I want to show it to you. Get your opinion. I don't want to move too fast, but honestly, I feel you are my future. I also don't want to assume that you will move here with me. I hope you do. I want you to have a decision and I'm hoping Logan's place will make your decision easier. You game to at least check it out?" he asks.

"Absolutely. Are we going there now?" I ask.

I'm excited to see Logan's house. I heard it was amazing. I'm not sure if the staff comes with it. I'm hoping not. I know Presley Ann was freaked out by how things seemed to get cleaned up by themselves. However, not having to do the tedious shit would be really cool.

We climb into Patrick's SUV and drive out of the downtown area. We head up and up and up, around curve after curve. In a way the scenery makes me feel like I'm back home. He pulls into a driveway that has a gate.

He puts in a code and the gates open and we again head up. I'm in awe at the size of the house. There's a four car garage that sits off to the side. The house seems to dip into the hillside.

We walk through the front door and I'm speechless. There's a slight entrance but once you step through, it's an open vast space. Windows are everywhere and it draws me forward to the ones facing the cliffs immediately.

"Wow," is all I can say. The views are breathtaking.

I feel his arm wrap around my waist, standing next to me, we look down onto LA. "Can you picture yourself looking at this in your future?"

"It's magical, Yes, I could get used to this. Oh my God, is that an infinity pool?" I say, opening up the doors and rushing outside.

Without even thinking, I toss my hat and start stripping down. I want to swim up to the edge. I've seen these online and have always wanted to experience one.

Once I'm down to my boxers, I run and jump into the deep end. I swim up to the edge and glance over the side. It's incredible. The city lights, the cliffside and the stars all mixed in. I think that I could handle living here.

I'm by myself, but it's only for a few minutes before I feel the water shift and feel Patrick up against me. He places his chin on my shoulder and places his arms on top of mine, intertwining our fingers against the edge.

"I love this," I say looking back with a smile.

"I love having you here and I love that you love it too. It's beautiful, right?" he asks.

"It is," I say as I turn and kiss his cheek.

Presley Ann was right when she said it was kind of freaky here. I never saw anyone, but when we get out of the pool, there are towels sitting on the edge of one of the lounge chairs.

I look inside and see that the table is set and there is food there.

"How did I not see all this happen?" I ask laughing as I dry off.

"Unfortunately, that doesn't come with the house, so don't get used to it," he says laughing.

We sit down in only our boxers to an amazing meal. We talk the whole time through eating. Laughing about our day and the things we did. We scan through each other's pictures and laugh. Today was so much fun.

I get to the last picture on his phone and see myself at the edge of the infinity pool. It's a really cool shot. I send it to myself and make it my profile picture.

"That is an amazing picture of you. I'm gonna save that shit and that will definitely be on the wall in a frame." He says.

"I would love to see that on a wall. I just wish we could have had someone take one with both of us out there," I say reaching out for his hand.

At that moment, Patrick's phone dings. He lifts it up and opens up the message and lets out a laugh.

"Well, it seems like your wish will be granted," he says showing me the message.

It seems that someone that is in the house but invisible took a shot of us. It's brilliant and set in black and gray.

I'm freaked out a little but can't help but shout out, "Thank you!"

I think I hear a soft, "Welcome," come from somewhere near the kitchen.

"I'm sorry. But that shit is weird and although I don't want anyone to lose their job if we keep them, they'll have to show themselves or I'll think this place is fucking haunted." I say looking around with a nervous smile.

We both hear giggling and Patrick says, "I agree. Mary? Can you come out and stop freaking out my boyfriend?"

A woman appears with a huge smile. "I'm sorry. I'm used to being discreet. I hope you don't mind that I took that picture. I just thought it was a magical moment, and I thought it was beautiful."

"Ma'am. It was extraordinary. Thank you," Patrick says. "It will definitely be one that gets printed and framed."

"I don't want to speak out of line, but if you do end up buying this house, I would love to stay on to help and I will adjust my rates. I will also promise not to be a ghost if you allow me," she says tucking her head and folding her hands in front of her.

"Mary. If I do buy this, I will do everything I can to keep you. But, yeah, I would like that you were more present and not hiding."

"Thank you. I would love to continue on here," she says. "You two have a good night."

"Bye, Mary," I say. "If we can afford it, we need to keep her."

Patrick laughs. "So, I guess you are considering moving here with me?"

"I guess I am," I say smiling.

Chapter Seventeen

Patrick

I wanted to see his reaction to Logan's house. I really want this to be our home. I just don't know if he's going to be acceptive to everything. Shit. I just want him to move here. Is that too much to ask?

When he jumps into the pool and swims to the edge, I saw my future. This is where I want him. This is where I need him. I just hope he stays. Eventually at least.

We have a great dinner and when Mary sends me the picture of us at the end of the pool, my heart soars. It's an incredible shot.

"I really love this house. It needs some color though," William says looking around. "I mean it's comfy and homey, just needs a pop here and there. Like a few pillows or something."

"If I buy it, I'll make sure you have full range to decorate," I say watching him closely for his reaction.

"It's so open. I can see hosting parties here. I love the open staircase. Is that a library up there?" he says without blinking an eye at my comment.

"Yeah, there's a big comfy oversized chair up there too. Yet, it's not closed off. Logan has an awesome book collection. He'll probably take those but he's leaving everything else that's not personal. It's move in ready," I say still looking intensely at him.

He looks at me and smiles. "It's perfect for you."

That's not exactly what I wanted to hear.

His smile gets bigger. "Tell me what is going on in that head. If I didn't know any better, I would think you are asking me to move out here and in here."

"It's crazy. I know," I say looking down. "It's probably too much to even ask and definitely way too soon."

"Is it? Any of it? Didn't we say to be honest with one another? Don't be afraid to say what you are thinking. I'll either shoot you down or I'll agree. Or we'll come up with an alternative. No games, Patrick. No fishing. Just say it," he says stretching out his hand and turning it face up.

I place my hand in his, "I can't stop thinking about making this ours. I've been watching you all night hoping you'd love it as much as I do. It's a lot to ask though."

"It is a lot to ask, but so would me asking you to move out with me. However, are we not working on establishing a forever type of relationship? It's not going to happen tomorrow, but we still need to talk about it. Talk about options so that a few months from now, a year from now, we have a plan. We are on one side of this fucking continent. Together." He responds.

"I love the mountains. I really do. I can see myself living there with you. My biggest fear is not being able to walk down the street and hold your hand. We can do that here. That's the only thing holding me back from moving tomorrow. You are right, though. I'm sorry for being evasive," I say tilting my head. "So, what are your thoughts?

"You know I love my mountains. My momma is there and all my friends," he says and my heart starts to beat.

I could move there. I really could. I don't really want to. To be honest, I just think the hiding would bother me too much and would cause an unnecessary strain. It's hard enough being gay in this world.

"I just saw your heart drop. I can see it in your eyes. Let me finish though. As I said I love my mountains, but just in one day, I've never felt this free. This accepted. This house is incredible. It's quiet and reminds me of home. That pool is badass. It's a viable option. I'm not saying no," he says standing up and pulling me to my feet. "We talk, discuss and weigh all our options. Agree?"

"Of course. I was scared. I'm sorry. It won't happen again," I say pulling him into a hug.

We opt not to stay the night since neither of us brought an overnight bag. I actually have stuff here in the spare bedroom for when I've had to stay a few days in the past. However, I want our first night in this house to be when it's ours.

When we finally get back to my apartment, we strip down naked and just fall into bed. We are both exhausted from the long day. We form a spoon. Him on the outside with his face tucked into my neck. I'm instantly so comfortable, I find myself drifting in and out of sleep.

"Love you, Doc," I whisper as I yawn.

"Love you too, babe," he says pulling me in closer and entwining our legs.

At this point, I don't care where we live. I just know that I need to be with this man every waking day and sleeping night of my life.

My feelings of comfort unfortunately, end the next morning.

Chapter Eighteen

Buddy

My phone continues to ding and wakes me. My heart starts pounding thinking something happened to my ma. I untangle myself from Patrick and grab it rolling to sit up on the side of the bed.

It's Facebook notifications. I take a deep breath and relax a little knowing it's not about mama, but what could it be?

Once I bring up one of the notifications, my heart starts pounding again. No. Fuck.

I'm livid. I'm scared. I don't know what to even fucking do as I roll through all the comments. A simple post that can change everything. I'm not ready. Why? I just sit on the side of the bed breathing hard and trying to reel in my emotions.

I feel Patrick stir as he tries to place his hand on my back, but I pull away. "Don't." That's all I manage to get out.

“What’s wrong?” he says immediately sitting up. He tries to get close again, but I stand up and toss my phone to the bed.

“How could you?” I say walking into the bathroom and closing the door.

I can’t even look at him right now. I feel like I’m going to be sick.

Chapter Nineteen

Patrick

I hear his phone dinging. He unwraps himself from me and sits up on the side of the bed. I can hear his breathing pick up. I try to reach out and touch him, but he pulls away. What is going on?

When I try to move closer, he stands up and drops his phone, going into the bathroom and closing the door. I don't want to cross any lines, but I need to know what the fuck is going on.

Picking up his phone, I see it. A picture I posted of us yesterday. It was innocent. So, I thought. I didn't notice that face recognition auto tagged him. We had just come out of the hat store. I took a picture of us together. The picture itself was simple. Two friends hanging out. However, the tags I put were pretty clear.

#myman
#forever
#truelove
#gayinLA

There were positive comments. There were a lot of negative ones. Fuck.

I've fucked this up. One simple post and I think I've just ended everything that I want and love in my life. How do I fix this?

I stand and walk over to the door of the bathroom. I hear him getting sick. I sink to the floor and press my body against the door and start to sob.

"I'm sorry. I'm so sorry. I didn't even notice that it tagged you. I would have never done that on purpose. Fuck, Doc. I fucked it all up," I practically yell. "Please talk to me."

I feel the door move and imagine that he's pressed up against the other side. An impasse of sorts. I literally feel my heart crack.

"How? How could you not notice I was tagged?" he says sounding defeated. "Did you read the comments, Patrick? I didn't want to come out that way. You took away my choice of how I wanted to do it. You may have thought you got what you wanted because I don't think I can even go home now. You didn't though because I want to be anywhere but here," he ends on a whisper.

"I didn't want anything. I never wanted to out you. It was an innocent fucking picture. Yes, the hashtags pushed it over the edge, but it was how I was feeling. I fucking love you," I say pounding my fist against the door. "Fuck!"

I wipe my face as I stand up. I calmly go and get dressed. I don't know what more I can do. I fucked up and I think I've lost the only person I've truly ever loved.

I grab my keys. I'm in a daze. I drop into my SUV and just drive. I have no idea where I'm going. I can't stop the tears and I can barely see. I end up pulling over at a lookout in the hills. Encircling my head in my hands against the steering wheel, I cry like I've never cried before.

I hear my phone ringing. At least I remembered to bring it. I don't remember much of anything else. I can't seem to catch my breath. I literally want to just run my car off of the cliff.

My phone continues to ring. I grab it and see that it's Mick calling. Taking a deep breath, I wipe my tears and answer.

"Patrick. Where are you?" he sounds panicked.

"I don't know," I say between breaths. "An overlook in the hills. I fucked up and lost him."

"Patrick. Listen to me. It's a hiccup. It may be a big one, but Buddy is worried." He says.

I look at my phone and see that I have numerous missed calls from him. I never even heard them.

"I don't know how to fix this. I'm scared, Mick. I love him so much."

"Go home. Talk to him. Man up, dude. You fucked up. Won't be the last time that happens. Fuck, you are two guys so I see a constant fuckory happening with you two. We are men and we fuck up constantly. You fix it with sex or something. Fuck if I know. Just go home and talk to him. Leaving him just makes it worse," Mick says.

"Okay. I'm heading there now. God. I'm so scared, Mick," I say.

"I'll call him and let him know you are coming and try to calm him down before you get there," Mick says. "Just keep saying you are sorry dude. Suck his dick or whatever you guys do," he says laughing.

"Fuck you, Mick," I say laughing.

I sit and look over the city. Taking a deep breath, I decide to call William. He answers immediately.

"Where are you?" he says.

"I'm sorry. I'm so sorry, baby." it's all I can say.

"I know," he sighs.

"I deleted the post. Too late, I know, but I didn't realize Doc. I really didn't," I say as I head back to my apartment.

"I know, Patrick. It's done. Come back and help me. I don't know what to do or what to say and I need your experience. I need you," he says.

I hear his pain and it's killing me.

I finally get to my apartment. I park my car and take a deep breath. He's willing to talk. He's not at the airport running. Instead, I was the one to run. I have to stop doing that. I need to own up to what I did and we need to face this together. How? I'm not sure. Knowing he is willing means more than anything right now. I may not have lost him after all.

I walk in and William is sitting on the couch. He stands and I can't help but immediately walk into him. When I feel his arms wrap around me, I start sobbing again. I tuck my face into his neck and just breathe him in.

"I love you. I don't want to lose you. I can't believe this happened. I would have never done that on purpose. I read some of the comments. Sorry. It's deleted now. What do you need me to do? How is your mom?" I'm trying to stay calm, but I'm freaking out.

"Mom is okay. She already knew and always said that I shouldn't hold back because of her. I know her friends though. I don't want her to lose the people in her life because of me. Although, she said that anyone that didn't accept me, she didn't want in her life, to begin with. I still feel like shit," he says rubbing my back and pulling me close.

He seems to be comforting me. Wow.

"You want my help? This isn't going to be easy, because I fucked up. It's out there, babe. So, it's really up to you at this point. You may be the one to have to do a post. I'll help you and I'll be there for you. I really think it has to come from you. I'm sorry. I know you aren't ready for this," I say pulling back and looking him in his eyes.

"I'm not. It had to happen sooner or later. I'm still really pissed at you for taking that choice away from me. However, you literally ripped the band aid off. I should probably thank you. I don't know when I would have gotten the courage to do it myself," he says shrugging a shoulder. "I'm thinking I need to do this on my own, maybe?"

"Okay. I'm going to take a shower. I really am sorry," I say giving him a quick kiss.

"I know. Welp, here goes everything," he says taking a seat at the kitchen table.

I stand and stare at him for a moment. He's so fucking handsome and I almost lost him.

After my shower, I see a few notifications on my phone. There's one that especially makes me smile bigger than I've ever smiled before.

Chapter Twenty

Buddy

I feel his eyes on me. I love his intensity. I can feel it deeply. I take a deep breath and start a post.

This was not how I wanted everyone to find out. I'm gay. There I said it. If you have been paying attention to my life, you would have realized that already. Missy Jo is my best friend. She was once my girlfriend, but that's awkward when you are gay. I love her. I truly do. For her to put her life on hold in order to protect me, I can never repay her. I will probably lose friends over this, but they were never my true friend if this is what ends it. The band aid has been ripped off. I'm scared, but I also feel a sense of relief. This has been something I've hidden all my life. Only my momma knew. Now I no longer have to hide. I no longer have to be fake. I can live my life how it should be lived. I found someone who makes me feel alive for the first time in my life. He just happens to be a man. The most wonderful man I've ever met. I ask that you respect my momma. If I hear differently, I will call your ass out. So be forewarned. I will be spending the next few days in LA with my boyfriend and we will be posting a lot of obnoxiously cute pics. Pictures of two people who have found each other against the odds and fell in love. I love you, Patrick. I can't wait to see what our future holds.

I leave out hashtags. I'm not about those. I go to my profile and change my status to "In a relationship" and tag Patrick.

The first comment is from Mick. It simply says, "I love you brother."

I know this is not going to be easy. The place I live in isn't one to be acceptive of my lifestyle. However, I already know I have people in my corner. Most importantly, my momma. She really is all that matters in the whole scheme of things. Patrick lost both of his parents by coming out. I couldn't image that.

I took a shower to try to compose myself earlier. So, I don't go in and join him, but I want him. I instead strip down and relax on the bed as I listen to the water being shut off. I hear him squeal and I laugh, knowing he saw my post and tag.

I lay on his bed and stroke myself while I wait, looking at the bathroom door. The door flies open and I see him holding his phone and smiling.

"I've never been tagged in a relationship. William, I'm honored. I don't even know what to say," he says setting his phone down on the nightstand. He drops his towel and crawls across the bed and straddles me.

“So, you liked it?” I say reaching up and pulling him down and pressing my lips against his.

“I loved it, and I love you,” he says smiling as he kisses me back.

“I turned my phone off. I don’t want any negative right now. I know I’m going to get it, but that’s on them and not you or me. I want to spend the next few days just experiencing life as I have never experienced,” I say rolling us over.

He wraps his legs around me and I feel his hard cock against me. Reaching down, I give it a quick tug. I suck the tender part right behind his ear and he thrusts up with a groan.

“Do you trust me?” I ask as I reach over and grab some lube.

“After everything we’ve been through. I trust you with everything,” he says spreading his legs and raising them up.

I reach down between us and press my fingers that are covered with lube against his ass. I continue to grind against him. Our cocks are side by side and pressed against each other’s stomachs.

I slowly insert two fingers gently lubing him. I still feel a bit of hurt and although I don't want to hurt him, I want him to feel a little bit of discomfort.

Lifting up and looking directly into his eyes, I rub my cock with lube and without any warning, I thrust forward breaking quickly through the breach of his ass. He lets out a grunt, breathing through his nostrils. His eyes flare but he smiles.

"Fuck me, William. Teach me a lesson for being bad. Fuck." He says leaning his head back and groaning.

I thrust forward and I'm fully seated. Patrick squeezes down on me and I almost see stars. "Fuck," I yell.

I wrap my arms around his legs and pull them further up towards his head. I'm able to grab his shoulders and pull him down as I surge up.

I bury my face into Patrick's neck as I continue to pound in and out. He matches my growls.

As good as it feels to take him raw and bare, a guilty feeling comes over me.

I slow my movements and release his legs. I move my hands to each side of his face. Continuing to move slowly, I kiss him.

"I'm sorry. I was too rough. I don't want to hurt you and I feel like I was taking my frustrations out on you."

"It's okay. I deserve it, but I love it. I want you to fuck me and make love to me. I want you unguarded. I want you raw. I want you at your worst and at your best, William," he says rolling us over.

We are still connected and he takes control. His knees are at my armpits. He continues to press down, taking me into him. Each time he slams down, I thrust up.

We keep rolling back and forth. Him on top, me on top, until I take the lead.

"You are mine. Never forget that" I say grabbing his cock and stroking as I thrust up and feel that familiar tingling in my balls.

"Come, Patrick," I say grinding and ready myself.

He grunts and I feel the wetness of his cum on my hand. I'm done. I push forward one last time as I let go. His ass squeezes, draining everything from me.

I groan as I continue to grind. "That was incredible."

“Best make up sex, I’ve ever had. Not that I have any to compare it to, but I feel like we need to fight more,” he says laughing.

His laughter pushes me out of him and I find myself laughing too.

“I don’t want to have make up sex. I don’t want to ever fight. I know that’s unrealistic, but I just want us to be happy and fuck. Is that too much to ask?” I say rolling off him and pulling him into my arms.

Chapter Twenty-One

Patrick

Drying off after showering, I can't help but look at my phone. I immediately read his post and smile. I'm so proud of him.

I then see my notifications and see that he tagged me as being in a relationship. I can't help but squeal. I dance around in a circle hugging my phone.

I can't wipe the smile off my face. When I walk out of the bathroom, William is laying on my bed. He looks so sexy laying there stroking his hard cock.

I drop my towel and immediately crawl across the bed and straddle him. When he asks if I trust him, I don't hesitate to answer yes.

I've never let anyone take me bare. I never realized how different it would feel. It was softer, warmer and intimate.

He took me hard and rough and then apologized. I loved it. There's something primal and sexy when taken that way.

I teased him about make up sex, but I agree that I don't want to fight ever again. My heart felt like it was literally being pulled from my chest today.

I roll over and kiss his chest. "I need to clean up. As much as I love having my ass filled with your cum, I feel like I'm going to do something that may not be very sexy."

"Fart bubble?" he says covering his face and laughing hysterically.

"Oh my God! That is so gross, but yes!" I say rolling over and running to the bathroom.

I try not to laugh because I just know what will happen.

I clean up the best I can without taking another shower and take a warm washcloth in to clean up William. Both our stomachs growl at the same time.

"I need to feed you. Come on. Let's get dressed and go to the little diner around the corner," I say.

We both get dressed and walk hand in hand down the sidewalk. "Thank you for being here. Thank you for not giving up on me even when I fucked up so bad."

“Let’s put that behind us. I was so mad, I’m not going to lie. But now that it’s over, I feel like a weight has been lifted. I’m out. I don’t have to hide anymore. I also really like it here. I didn’t think I would. I enjoy Logan’s place more than in the city though. Just to be honest.” William says looking over at me and making a face.

“So, you would consider moving here? You know I have land waiting for me in Tennessee as well? I love LA, but I would be willing to move. You know that right? For you,” I say smiling. “We don’t have to make any major life decisions right now.”

“I know. I think one major life event in one day is enough. I don’t want to go home though, just saying,” He says as we reach the diner and my phone starts ringing.

I pull it out of my pocket and see a number I don’t recognize, right before I go to hit decline, William grabs it and answers putting it on speaker.

“Momma? He says looking at me with worry.

“Well good lawd boy. I’ve been tryin’ to call you all mornin’. I had to call Presley Ann to get Patrick’s number. Do you want this ol’ coot to die from worry?” she says and I can’t help but laugh at her dramatics.

"I'm sorry. I turned off my phone. I guess you saw the post? Are you okay? I should have called you. I got caught up in my self and wasn't thinkin'." He says. He has an accent, but it seems to get heavier when he's talking to his mother.

"Momma, you're on speaker. Be nice," he says smiling.

"I will do none of the sort. You had me scared. You come out on social media without warnin'. Those city folk need to hear this," she laughs and says, "I'm glad you are okay Buddy. I'm proud of you, baby. Patrick, you take care of my boy. You will have the same wrath he gets if anything happens." She says sending her love as we both return ours and hang up.

"Woo wee, she's a spit fire," I say laughing. "I'll have to remember to make sure I call her and keep her updated."

"I should have called her. I feel horrible. She likes you though, so at least you have that," he says laughing. "Now feed me."

Laughing we head into the diner, it feels like the beginning of the rest of our lives.

Chapter Twenty-Two

Buddy

The rest of the week was wonderful. Waking up beside Patrick is something I want to do forever. I haven't told him yet, but I've already looked online for therapist positions. Seems LA has more than a few openings. I'm not really surprised. I could probably open my own practice and have a full schedule in a short amount of time. I'm not sure I'm ready for that though.

I put in a few applications and have already gotten a few responses. I have one more day here and interviews set up for most of that time.

I wanted to spend it with him. However, when I tell him, I'm sure he'll be more than happy to let me take them. I figured out how to sync my phone to his printer and printed out the interview schedule.

When my alarm that I set goes off, Patrick stirs and starts slamming his fist on the nightstand. I laugh and pull him over to me and whisper, "go back to sleep. It's mine and I have a surprise."

"Mmmm. I love surprises," he sighs and rolls over smiling and hugging his pillow.

I make him breakfast and grab the schedule off of his printer. I smile remembering the conversation with my Ma. I called and had it approved by her first, this time.

Her last words to me were, "I want you to soar. Spread those wings baby. That's all I've ever wanted. I'm so happy that you are happy. Baby boy, your happiness is all that matters to me. I love you so much and I'm so proud of the man you are becoming."

I put the food on a tray and slip the calendar between the mug of coffee and plate. He starts on the coffee and hums. He sees the calendar and picks it up looking at it with one eyebrow raised.

When he realizes what the calendar means, the smile on his face is one that I will never forget.

"Is this what I think it is?" he asks. "Are these interviews?"

"Yeah, I'm sorry that I can't spend my last day with you," I say.

"But you get to spend your life with me. That's better, Doc," he says smiling. "That so much better. Tell me you talked to your mom though, please. I don't want her wrath."

"Yes, damn straight I talked to her. She gave me her blessing," I say smiling.

"I'm so happy. Thank you, Doc. I mean, I couldn't have dreamed of a better day," he says giving me a kiss.

"I love you and I really do love it here. Wish me luck," I say as I start to dress for my interviews.

He sets the tray on the nightstand and gets out of bed. Helping me straighten my tie, he says, "You are so incredibly handsome. I'm the luckiest man in the world."

"I'm just as lucky. I'll call you in-between," I say as I take his SUV and head off to my first interview.

After the third, I had made my decision, but I want to go to them all, just in case. Two practices made me immediate offers, but one was way above what I expected. No one else came even close.

I explained that I had a few other interviews, but that I would let them know before the end of the day.

After the last one, I'm exhausted but sure of my decision. When I call and accept the one offer, I was given a month to make the move. I was going to be in a partnership with one other therapist. He already had patients that he needed me to take. He asked me if I could stop back to fill out some paperwork since he knew I was leaving.

Two hours later, I had a few file folders with patient information that I could review and get familiar with. I was beyond excited.

I was also scared as shit. This wasn't something to be taken lightly. This was a huge life change. HUGE!.

My mind started drifting to the "what ifs". I didn't even realize I had pulled into a parking spot at Patrick's apartment. I just sat in his SUV and gripped the steering wheel.

What if it doesn't work out? What if I get out here and then we break up and I have to move back home? We've known each other for almost a year, but we've really only been together for a few months.

Am I making the right decision?

I hear my mom's voice in my head, "Soar baby boy."

Taking a deep breath, I send up a prayer. "Lord. Let me know that I'm making the right choice here. Please?"

I jump when someone knocks on the window.

"Are you alright? Did it not go well?" Patrick asks.

I've never seen someone's eyebrows be so on point. I've also never thought of eyebrows as being sexy, but Patrick's are spot on perfect.

I shake my head and grab my messenger bag from the front seat and get out.

"Awww, babe. It's okay. I'm sure there will be other opportunities," he says pulling me in for a hug.

Was that my sign? It had to be my sign. I mean, I asked and immediately Patrick was here.

I hug him back and take in his delicious cologne. "Can you wait for a month?"

"What do you mean?" he asks leaning back and grabbing my shoulders.

"I got an offer. I start in a month," I say tilting my head and giving him a small smile.

"But? You are worried about the decision. I can understand that. It's a big one. Not to be taken lightly. It's also a decision that you alone have to make. You know how I feel. You know that I want you here more than anything in the world. You also know that I'd move there too in a heartbeat. You know I could since Logan is there. It just makes more sense to me for you to be here. To be where we are more accepted," he says giving me a soft kiss.

"I love that we are accepted here, too. Patrick, I was so sure when I accepted that it was what I wanted. Then those flutters of doubt crept into my head. I heard momma's voice telling me to soar, and I sat in the car just praying for a sign. Then you knocked," I say reaching up and taking his face in my hands. "You were the sign. You are my future and my forever. I know this deep in my soul."

"Let's celebrate," he says pulling out his phone and calling to make reservations for dinner. "You'll love this place. It's next to impossible to get in, but I have connections."

We head up to his apartment and take a shower together. We take turns washing each other. It's so sensual. We end up jacking each other off at the same time. With slippery hands, our mouths and tongues search each other until we both release.

We dry each other off and it's playful and fun. Patrick runs gel through his hair and then runs it through mine, giving me a little style to my hair. I look in the mirror and say, "Damn, I look hot."

Laughing, we get dressed together. It's something that I can picture as being a normal routine of ours.

He drives us up the hills to a restaurant that looks incredible. A valet comes and takes the keys. Patrick wraps his arm around me once he meets me on the other side of the car and we walk in.

The hostess greets us with a smile and immediately takes us to a table outside overlooking the city. The view is breathtaking.

"I think this is my new favorite place and I haven't even tasted the food," I say looking around.

"Well, the food is to die for. I love this place. I've been wanting to bring you here but wanted to wait. I can't think of a better time," he says reaching out and grabbing my hand.

Patrick was right. The food was the best I've ever had.

Chapter Twenty-Three

Patrick

When William left, I didn't hesitate to call Logan. I pray that his interviews go well, but I don't want to wait. Logan agrees to sell me his house and even though I try to fight him, he set it up to give me a fantastic deal.

This is a multi-million dollar home. Even though I make really good money, I'm nowhere at the level of Logan. I would never be able to afford his house. Not in my wildest dreams. I try to argue with him on being realistic, but he says he wants me to have it.

"Patrick. Listen to me. I know I could make a lot of money selling the house to someone else, but I don't want anyone else to have it. I want you and Buddy to have it. It would make me happy. You aren't getting it for free. You are getting it at a good price and one that I think is fair. Because you will be happy and that makes me happy. Plus, I know my home will be well taken care of and one that I can visit when Presley Ann and I come out there," he says.

"You are one of the most incredible men I've ever met. Thank you, brother," I say already thinking of things I want to change.

"Thank you, brother, for loving my home just as much as I did. You deserve it. I hope Buddy's interviews go well. Keep me posted," he says.

"Shit, I do too. I'm so excited," I respond.

"Me and Pip are excited for you too. See you soon," he says as we hang up.

The day dragged. I took a run. I took a shower. I watched some brainless TV. I got a few texts to let me know what he was doing. The last text said he was done and he was heading back. That was a half hour ago. Traffic is horrible here so I'm not concerned, but I go to the window and look out anyways.

I see my SUV parked and William sitting behind the wheel. He is sitting there with a dead look on his face. I grow concerned as I look and he still doesn't move.

I walk out and knock on the window and startle him. He grabs his messenger bag and gets out of the car. I immediately pull him into my arms and tell him that it's going to be okay.

I assume the interviews didn't go well. To my amazement, he tells me that he actually received an offer and accepted. One month and he will be here with me.

My heart pounds with excitement.

"I didn't know if it would go well or not, but I had hoped. I talked with Logan earlier today and we've worked out a deal on his house. So, when you come back, we will be moving into our house," I say still running everything through my head.

"Wow. Our house. There's so much I need to do. How much do I bring? How do I get it here? I'm excited but I'm feeling overwhelmed," he says.

"One or two boxes at a time. Logan already said we have full use of his plane. Let's not worry about that now though. Let's celebrate," I say pulling out my phone and calling my favorite restaurant.

It's the one that I wanted to bring him to and as I'd hoped, he loved it.

He's leaving me tomorrow. I'm not looking forward to it. However, I know he will be back and for good. I can make it through one month.

We don't make love that night. Instead, we talk, plan and laugh until the sun comes up. This is how I know this is right. It's not about sex. I could spend all night just talking with him. He's so incredible to be around. I really enjoy just being with him. We end up falling asleep wrapped into each other's arms. The alarm goes off and I groan.

"Damn it. I know you will be back, but I don't want to let you go," I say pulling him close.

"I feel the same. It will crawl and it will fly. We are just a phone call or video chat away. I love you so much, Patrick," he says kissing me softly.

It's a slow kiss. It's a passionate kiss. It's a kiss that says, "I love you." A kiss that says, "You are mine. Forever."

I've never felt so many emotions in a kiss. It's an everlasting moment that will be forever engraved into my brain. A moment of clarity. He's my future.

Taking him to the airport, we talked and held hands the whole way.

"I don't want you to change anything in the house. The only thing I want is to make it ours with personal items from both of us. Oh, and some big pillows with lots of color for the couch," he says laughing.

"Shit, yes. That couch is amazing but sooo boring," I say in a sing song voice.

I unload his luggage from the trunk and we embrace at the curb. "I love you, Doc. I'll be counting down the days."

"Same. I'll call when I land," he says, giving me a strong hug and a kiss.

I stand at the curb until I see him disappear. I struggle not to cry but I suck in a breath and smile knowing it won't be long.

I spend the rest of the afternoon setting up a moving company. I grab my luggage out of my closet and throw in a bunch of clothes. I have some already at Logan's, no, my house, but I need more.

One suitcase full of clothes and another one full of personal items, I head to the hills.

Mary greets me at the door, "Welcome home."

"Come with me to the kitchen," I say grabbing her hand.

"I'm not going to be able to keep the staff that Logan did. Unfortunately, they will have to be let go, but Logan assures me that he will find them jobs. However, this is your house too and I would be more than honored if you would stay on. I may have to cut back on some of your hours, but I can't imagine you not being here," I say giving her a hug.

"I'm so happy to hear that. I was so scared to have to leave this house. Seeing you and William was amazing. I will never invade your privacy ever again, I hope you know that. I was worried that you would let me go after that," she says.

"Hell no. I'm getting that picture you took edited and framed and putting that bitch right up there over that fireplace," I say laughing.

"I'll proudly help you hang it," she says. "Are you hungry?"

"No, I'm good. Thank you," I say setting my suitcase with my personal items on the couch and open it. "I could use some help setting up these pictures and things around to make this feel more like mine."

"Let's do it," she says picking up a photo of me and Logan. "Well, this isn't good. There's already a picture of you two around here.

She smiles and holds up a finger, moving to the hall closet. Pulling out a square box, she comes over and hands it to me. "Housewarming present."

I tilt my head and pull open the top of the box. I see some Styrofoam on the top. I pull it out and see wood. It looks like a frame.

I look at her as my excitement builds. "No way."

Slowly I pull out a framed photo. It's black and white and it's the one. The one she took that night. William and I's silhouette, in the pool, overlooking the valley. There's a wash out of lights that appear to be orbs. It's breathtaking.

"Oh my God, Mary. How?" I ask.

"As soon as I took it, I knew I needed to get it edited and framed. I was going to wait to give it to you for your wedding, but when Logan called and said you were moving in, I pushed to get it done. I knew you would probably move in the first chance you had, so I'm glad that it was done today," she says. "Do you like it?"

"I love it. It's perfect," I say holding up the thirty-six by twenty-four framed print.

I immediately go to the fireplace and pull down the art deco print Logan had hung, replacing it with the print.

I put my arm around Mary and admire the masterpiece. "Thank you. I can't wait for William to see it."

"You're very welcome. I'm going to head out for the night, but I'll be back in the morning. Let me know if there is anything you need. Are you working tomorrow in the office or here?" she asks.

"I'll be here. I have the day off, so I'm going to be doing some reorganizing and making this mine," I say smiling.

"Well, movers have already started to pack up Logan's personal items to move to Tennessee. They will be here tomorrow to finalize. The office is packed, so you may want to start there. I'll be here to help do any cleaning that may need to be done. Have a wonderful night, and I look forward to working for you," she says.

"Thank you, Mary. See you tomorrow," I say.

I look around and find myself just standing in the living room and looking at that picture. It's so captivating. My phone buzzes and I see that it's William calling.

"Hey, babe. Miss you," I say.

"Yeah, I'm almost home. I miss you too. I'm going to probably sleep all day tomorrow to try to adjust to the time change. Thank goodness I had the sense to take an extra day," he says.

"I couldn't wait. I packed up some stuff and came over to Logan's, I mean our house," I say chucking.

"He's already had movers packing up his stuff. I got the ball rolling and movers on my set for two weeks from now. I'm going to sell most of the stuff. Since this one comes practically with everything. Oh, and Mary agreed to stay on. She helped me hang my first artwork and I can't wait for you to see it," I say walking up the stairs to the bedroom.

"Twenty-nine days, fourteen hours, and thirty-two seconds and I'll be there," he says.

"Tick tock, motherfucker, hurry up," I say as I hear him laugh.

"I'm pulling in now. I love you, Patrick." He sighs.

"I love you too, Doc."

I look around at what used to be Logan's bedroom and instead of the heartache I used to feel, knowing that man would never be mine, I feel a renewed sense of comfort. This is going to be where my life begins with William. Our oasis. Where all the magic is going to happen. I start to grow hard just thinking of all the amazing sex we are going to have in here.

I notice a card on the nightstand and go over and open it. It's a housewarming card from Logan. I stand and glance over his words, but tears form before I can even start to read.

I wipe my face with my hands and read the card out loud. He's so amazing.

Patrick,

I thought it may be weird to sleep on my mattress, so I replaced it with one of those fancy temperature and firmness control ones. I wish you happiness in your life with Buddy. Love you brother. I couldn't be happier that you finally found yours. I know what it's like. I've always wanted that for you. Funny how life happens and brings people in that end up being your soulmate. I believe I was meant to take that sabbatical. Not only for me, but for you too.

Sappy shit. Blah, blah blah. Love you, man,

Logan

I'm laughing and crying at the same time. I know it's late but I should call him anyway, just to be a dick. I decide not to and just strip down and crawl under the freshly washed sheets and comforter.

I'm home. All I need to be complete is William.

Chapter Twenty-Four

Buddy

I grab my suitcase from the carousel and start to walk out, when I see Mick and Marissa. They both give me a hug and we head out to Mick's truck.

"So, anything happen while I was gone?" I say in the back of the cab.

"Besides, you coming out and being the talk of the town. Not really," Mick says looking in the rearview mirror, for my reaction.

"Yeah, and what are they saying?" I ask, not really knowing if I want to hear it or not.

"It's actually not as bad as you would think. I mean all the guys are fine. They already suspected. Missy Jo wasn't exactly a good decoy. There just wasn't any chemistry between you two other than friends," Mick says chuckling. "The older folk, well that's another story. I know this will get your feathers in a ruffle, but your mom was kicked out of the book club. Before you get all worked up though, she started her own book club and took half the members with her."

"She gained a few too," Marissa says laughing. "Me and Presley Ann joined. That momma of yours has some interesting choices in books."

"Christ, don't tell me," I say laughing. "That's good to hear though. I knew my momma was strong."

"Buddy, there is something else. We had to clean up your townhouse door, it seems not everyone is as accepting," Mick says punching his steering wheel. "Stupid fucks left the spray cans though and it wasn't hard to get prints. They are in custody."

"Even more of a reason to move," I say with a sigh.

"We heard and we're really happy for you. Sad for us. At least we will have a place to go for vacation," Mick says.

"I'm sorry if I don't really want to hang out, guys. I'm plum tuckered from the time change. Come over for dinner tomorrow and we can catch up then," I say as Mick pulls into my complex.

I can see my door has been painted. "Hope you like the color, Marissa picked it out," Mick says as I get out.

"Don't really care, Mick. Won't me mine in a few weeks anyway," I say grabbing my stuff and heading up.

I had called Patrick from Mick's truck, so I just fall to the bed and sigh. I'm thankful that I took tomorrow off because all I want to do is sleep.

∞ ∞ ∞

I go into work and drop the news. My partners are disappointed but happy for me. My patients are not as happy. I had two break downs until I was able to get the therapist that was replacing me to calm them down. I stood at the side and watched, pleased that I knew they were going to be in good hands.

I gave two weeks to do the full transition. This will give me a week to pack and a week to relax before I start my new job.

Two weeks go by fast. The time difference sucks, but Patrick and I manage to video chat as much as possible. We even have a little sexy time every now and then.

I'm not taking any of my furniture, none of my kitchen shit and no bathroom stuff. I practically give it away to my friends. I had to laugh at them arguing over towels. I have a few boxes with my personal items that are stacked in the living room.

I'm on a blow up mattress for the next few nights. My back is killing me but I'm excited to get the hell out of here. I stopped into one of the local stores to get some food to carry me over the next few days and was so uncomfortable.

Normally, I would get greetings and stopped to have a few conversations, but instead, it was like I had the plague. I even had people hurry to other aisles to avoid me.

I no longer feel welcomed in the only town I've ever known. How sad is that?

I spend as much time as I can with momma. I cry every time I have to leave. She only smiles and continues to praise me on how proud she is of me. "Soar, baby boy."

My last night, the guys give me a going away party. Even momma came. We all hang out at Logan and Presley Ann's and have an early Thanksgiving feast.

Just as we are about to sit down, the door bursts open. "Bitches better not think they are having a feast without me." Patrick.

I rush over and pull him into my arms. He jumps up and wraps his legs around me and I just start crying and laughing. My emotions are all over the place.

"You're here," I say not caring who's watching as I give him a kiss.

"Of course, I am. The plane was coming to get you, so why wouldn't I be on it too?" he says kissing me back.

"You never said anything," I say as he drops his legs to the floor, still in an embrace.

"Surprise!" he says laughing.

We all sit down and have an amazing dinner. I couldn't be happier. I'm surrounded by my family. Not all are by blood, but family none the less.

That wasn't the only surprise we got that night. Presley Ann announces that she is pregnant, and Marissa announces she is as well.

"We are adding to our little family. It's so amazing and so incredible. I love each and every one of you, even the ones being grown. Thank you for tonight. Thank you for your acceptance and love. I'm going to miss you all, but when the little ones are born, we'll be here. I can't wait to meet them," I say raising my glass of wine. "To family. To healthy babies and to continued happiness."

"Here, here!" Patrick shouts.

"Seriously, this is incredible. I'm so happy I could cry, but I want you all to know that I appreciate your support of Patrick and me. I swear, if it wasn't for all of you, I may not have found the strength to do what I am doing. My coming out wasn't conventional, but with Patrick, who could expect that shit. He is my love. I don't care who accepts it, but love that you all do. It means so much to me. I would be lost in this world without each and every one of you. And momma, thank you for always having my back and being the badass momma I always knew you were. I love you all," I say taking another drink and hearing the cheers around the table.

My friend, Bug, suddenly stands and clears his throat, "Hey ya'll. I need to say something." The table grows silent. "I've known Buddy since we were babies. Our friendship never wavered through the years. He's been the most supportive, no offense to the others, of me and my struggles. I grew up with my mawmaw and pap. I didn't have it easy. But Buddy was always there. I know that the groceries that would suddenly appear on our porch were from him and his momma. When he was in college, he would still come by and make sure we were taken care of. I knew when he got his first job that those bills that were suddenly paid, were not by the grace of God, but because of him. He was always there. When he came out, my grandparents were shocked. They at first were appalled, but then, my mawmaw said something so incredible. She said, "he's still Buddy".

"You are Buddy. My friend, my savior and one of the most important friends I've ever had. I will always be grateful to you and your Ma for everything you did for me and my family. I only wish the best for you and Patrick," he says raising his glass and taking a drink.

I walk around the table and we embrace. I never knew he knew it was us that helped him. That doesn't even matter. Through everything, he accepts me.

I look around the table as people wipe the happy tears from their eyes and realize I'm crying as well.

These are the moments that reconfirm I'm a good person. It doesn't matter who I love. Being loved and accepted by the ones that are my tribe, that matters. Tonight, I feel loved. I'm so ready to move forward with Patrick and discover what I know will be the most incredible journey. One of love. Pure and untarnished.

Chapter Twenty-Five

Patrick

I can't believe he was surprised. I mean, I have access to the jet. Of course, I was going to come with it. I wanted to be here and I wanted to be with him for his last night.

His friends are pretty badass. I know their acceptance is so important to William and they didn't disappoint. I also knew he was special. But when I heard Bug's story, I didn't realize how special he was. He has done so much for his friends.

When the evening is over and we go to leave, I hug Logan and Presley Ann. Each whispers their own little piece of love in my ear. These are truly special friends.

I can't help but press my hand against both Presley Ann and Marissa's stomachs. It's something that I'll never experience. I want a child, but I know being a gay man, it's not something that is in the cards for me.

It's not impossible, I know that. Others have done it, but I know it's not easy. Hell, heterosexual couples can't even seem to catch a break.

All the hugs are given, and we are about to leave when William's mom pulls me aside.

She takes my face into her hands and smiles, " Thank you, Patrick. I know you meant no harm in your post. You did my boy a favor, though. I don't think he would have come out. At least not right away. I know he feels free now. I see the love between you two just by the way you look at each other. Take care of my boy out there. Or I'll come out there and kick your ass."

I tense up and she let's out a laugh. "I'm not sure if you are kidding or not, but I promise to take care of him. Although, I think he will more likely take care of me. He's the strong one."

"Yes, my baby is strong. I may or may not have been kidding," she smiles and taps my cheek softly. "I expect you two home for Christmas. No arguments."

"Yes ma'am, of course," I say loving how strong this woman is and how scared she has me right now.

Kissing my cheek, she gives me a warm embrace and I sink into her. It's a mom hug and I've missed having those.

"Call me ma or momma, son. I expect weekly calls from just you. I want to hear what's really going on with my boy and he tends to sugar coat things. I feel like I'll get the honest truth from you," she says squeezing me. "Plus, I would really like to get to know the man that makes my boy the happiest I've ever seen him."

"I would love that, ma," I whisper, testing calling her ma out loud. It feels good and right.

"Good boy. Stop over and say goodbye before you leave, okay?" she says giving me another hug.

"We will," I say.

On the way home, William asks what his mom and I talked about. When I tell him, he let's out a big laugh. "Good ol' ma."

"I promised to call her. I can't tell you what it means for her to accept me. I haven't had a mother figure in my life for a very long time," I say.

"She knows, but she wouldn't do it if she didn't truly care. She's also a very good judge of character," he says smiling over at me.

When we make it to his townhouse, I see the blow up mattress on his floor and the boxes stacked up in the corner.

"Oh hell no. The mattress on the plane is better than this shit. Pack up the truck, I'm calling Smitty. We are spending the night on the plane," I say grabbing a box.

Chapter Twenty-Six

Buddy

I start laughing and say, "It's not that bad," as a pang hits my back. "Well, maybe a little."

We get all the boxes in my truck and make our way to the airport. We are let onto the tarmac without any questions and park right beside the plane.

"Smitty is going to have some men pack the boxes in the plane. Let's go," he says sliding out.

All the lights are on and the steps are down. "Can we really do this?" I ask as a tall man approaches.

"You must be William, nice to meet you. Patrick, thanks for kicking me out, dude." Smitty says with a big smile. .

"I'm sorry. It wasn't my idea," I say.

"Logan has wanted me to stay with him and Presley Ann so it worked out, they were happy to have me stay the night at their place." He says shaking my hand.

"It's not a problem. We will have your stuff loaded and I'll be back in the morning," he says as he takes off.

"Oh, hey. I need to see my momma before we take off tomorrow," I say as he's leaving.

"That's fine. I'll be sure to wait for you. I have clearance to leave around noon, so just make sure you are back before then," he calls back. "Make sure you raise the steps, Patrick."

"Aye, Aye, Captain," he responds running up the steps. "Come on!"

I run up after him and look around at the amazing layout of the plane. There are a few captain's chairs, a few tables, and a few lounges. It's cozy. He hits a button and the stairs start to raise.

"Thank God I'm not claustrophobic," I laugh. "There's a bed in here? What if I have to pee?"

"There's a full bathroom and bedroom right back here. Bossman only has the best. And it's one of the perks of my job. I'll never quite get used to it, but I'll always enjoy it when I can."

"This is sweet!" I say looking around.

"It's small, but it's better than a fucking blow up mattress. Your back has to be killing you," he says rubbing his hands together. "Strip down and let me give you a massage."

I smile and quickly strip down to my boxers. Laying down on the bed I let out a sigh. "Oh wow, this is so comfy."

I'm on my stomach as I feel Patrick gently massage my feet. It feels incredible. He runs his hands up my calves and crawls onto the bed. With a fist to the center of my lower back, he applies pressure and I groan.

He rotates his fist and travels up my spine. He flattens his hand between my shoulder blades, applying pressure again. I'm about to fall asleep. He continues to massage my neck and shoulders and I feel like mush.

"Good?" he asks.

"So good," I sigh.

"So do you want to watch a movie?" he asks rolling over and propping himself on his elbow with his head in his hand.

"How?" I say rolling over and mimicking him.

"Oh, hon. This plane has wi-fi and satellite," He says grabbing a remote out of a side table drawer.

I see a TV almost as big as the wall at the foot of the bed. He turns it on and pulls up a movie but pauses it.

"Hold on. We need snacks," he says crawling over me and jogging down the plane. I feel the movement and laugh.

Coming back, he has a few bags of chips and a couple of beers, "Okay, ready."

"It's like camping, except with major amenities," I say as I pop open a beer and take a swig. "Maybe we should just quit our jobs and go jet setting around the world."

"That would be a dream come true, but Logan might not be so accepting of it. Gas prices are outrageous these days. I can only get away with so much. But one can dream. Where would you want to go first?"

"Hmmm. In this plane? Australia or New Zealand. I've always wanted to go, but I couldn't imagine spending all that time on a plane. But this plane, yeah, I would be fine," I say laughing.

"Maybe one day," he says smiling.

I look at the TV and see he pulled up a show about a group of friends in Canada. It's hilarious. We stop talking and binge watch the show until we both fall asleep.

I wake to my cock being stroked. I groan and stop his movements because I have to pee. "Love it, hold on."

I jump up and relieve myself to come back and find him on his stomach grinding the bed. His hands are pressed against the wall in front of him. He looks back at me and raises an eyebrow.

I see a bottle of lube on the side table and quickly grab it. Crawling on the bed, I lube up my cock and reach under him to rub his hard cock. I trail down until I cup his balls. He presses himself against my hand. I gently squeeze and continue up until I find his ass.

I squeeze more lube onto him and watch as it hits the top of his ass and runs down his crack. "Fuck me, Doc."

I spread his legs wide with my knees. Lining my cock up, I gently push forward until I'm fully seated. I take a deep breath because it's been a while and being bare, I find myself feeling the euphoria of wanting to just come.

"You need to move, Doc," he says pressing against me and grinding.

"Fuck," I moan.

I move slowly. In and out. Feeling everything. Patrick slaps his hand against the wall. "Fuck me, Doc."

I grab his hips and lift him onto his knees. I push forward with more strength as he pushes back. I press against his back and reach around to grab his cock that throbs in my hands.

With my free hand, I reach forward and press it against his one on the wall. I continue to push forward feeling him squeezed down.

"I'm going to come, babe," I say grinding my teeth.

"Don't stop," he says moving one of his hands down to wrap around the one I have on his cock.

He speeds up my strokes and looks back at me with such lust that I can't hold it any longer. "I can't...hold...it."

I feel his ass squeeze as his cock starts to pulse and I feel him coming. I let go and see stars. I press down and grind out my release.

"Fuck!" I shout.

I come hard. His ass continues to pulse around my cock and I can't stop thrusting forward. Every time we come together it's something special. I collapse on him with my hand still wrapped around his cock. It's still pulsing and I'm still pulsing in his ass.

He finally squeezes me out and my softened cock lays between his legs. I roll over and press my eyes together trying to catch my breath.

“Well, I guess we have sheets to wash.” He says laughing.

“Yeah, I don’t know if you are already, but one of the things on my bucket list is being a part of the mile high club. So, we may want to wait,” I say laughing.

“I’m not, but we will both be after this flight,” he says rolling over and pulling me into a deep kiss.

“I love you,” I sigh.

“I love you so much,” he says.

“Best words ever,” pulling him closer and kissing him.

Chapter Twenty - Seven

Patrick

I love William's mom. I love that she allows me to call her mom right off the bat. I love that she treats me like a son. I just simply love her and I love her son.

Our visit is short, but so warm and inviting. I hug her tight and walk away to allow William to have some privacy to say his goodbyes.

His face is full of tears when he finally makes it to the truck. I look and see his mom pressing her fingers against her lips as tears flow down as well. I can't help but run to her and pull her into my arms.

"I will take care of him and I will bring him home to visit. Promise," I say wiping her tears and kissing her cheek.

"I know you will, and this is what's best for him. I'm just going to miss him. You know," she says smiling through her tears.

"I know. Thank you for giving me your trust and for bringing up an amazing son. Thank you for all your acceptance. Love ya, Ma," I say giving her another hug.

"Love you too, son," she says patting my back.

I head back to the truck and climb in. William takes a deep breath and sighs. "She loves you. Thank you for going to her."

"I love her too and I did it for me, just as much as her. She fills a void for me," I say wiping my own tears.

"Oh, Patrick. I didn't even think about that. I'm glad I get the chance to share her. She has enough love to go around," he says grabbing the back of my neck and pulling me over into him.

"She's pretty damn amazing. I promised to take care of you and to bring you home as often as I can," I say laying my head on his shoulder.

"Let's get our lives started," he says kissing my temple.

"I'm ready," I say.

Mick and Marissa are at the airport to meet us. They are going to take William's truck and put it up for sale. We form a group hug.

"This isn't goodbye, guys. Until we see each other again," William says.

We get on the plane and settle in for takeoff. As soon as we hit altitude to be able to move around, William looks at me and winks.

"Ready to join the club?" he asks running to the back of the plane.

∞ ∞ ∞

Once we get to the house, I'm excited to see his reaction to our photo. He drops the bags and walks to the center of the living room.

"I like what you've done so far. Oh wow," he says as he notices the picture.

"Mary had it blown up as a housewarming present. Do you like it?" I ask walking over and wrapping my arms around him from behind. I rest my chin on his shoulder and look at the amazing black and white hanging above the fireplace.

"It's breathtaking. I can't believe that's us. I'm exhausted but I really want to take a swim. Real quick?" he says reaching back and pressing his hand against my face.

"As you wish," I say laughing.

"You always know exactly what to say," He laughs.

We both go running as we strip down. Clothes are being thrown as we go. He lets out a yell as he jumps in and I do as well, following him in.

We immediately swim to the edge and rest our arms on the side taking in the lights of the city below.

"Welcome home, Doc," I say laying my face on my forearm and looking over at him.

He mimics me and smiles. "Great to be home, Patrick."

Chapter Twenty-Eight

Buddy

I love the picture. I love how I instantly felt like I was home. I have a pool. An infinity pool that looks over the city. I didn't think I would like it. I'm a country boy, but we are so far away from the city. It's like we are on top of the world looking down.

When we crawl into bed, he shows me Logan's note and I smile. "It's really comfortable. He's a great friend."

We snuggle close. He left the doors open to the balcony that is off the bedroom. There's a nice breeze blowing and I smell the fresh outside. The air is different than back home, but it's still the outdoor smell that pulls me into loving this even more. I think he knew this and I love that he is trying to make this more comfortable for me. I take in a deep breath.

"I'm home, Patrick. Thank you for trying to make me feel comfortable. You don't have to try anymore. I've never felt more at home than when I'm lying here in your arms. You are my home. No matter where we are. And shit, we have a fucking fabulous pool," I say laughing.

"That we do. I want you to make this your home though. In the next week, you have off before you start work, you have free reign to do what you want. I want your touches on our home too." He says yawning.

"I will. I don't see anything I want to change. Yet," I snicker. "Tomorrow is another day."

"I have to head into the office early, babe. I love you but I need to sleep and this fucking jet lag is going to kick my ass," he says snuggling in deeper.

We kiss softly and exchange our love. I fall asleep excited to explore tomorrow.

When I wake, there is a note on Patrick's pillow.

Hey Doc. There's a lot of rooms in this house. Pick one for your office and get Mary to help get what you need. I also know you will need a vehicle. She will have a few options for you to look into. I'll be home around six and I would love for us to just talk about what you want to do. Love you, Patrick

I smile and roll out of bed and take a shower. When I get downstairs, Mary is in the kitchen and has breakfast for me.

"I'm not used to this, Mary. I'm sorry. I appreciate everything you are doing, but it's just weird to me," I say.

"I completely understand. I'm here for you, but I will never overstep and I never want to make you uncomfortable."

"Thanks, Mary. This house is so huge. I don't even know where to start." I love it, don't get me wrong. It feels like home even in its vastness.

"I was supposed to help with your office. So, I'm going to make a suggestion. There's one room upstairs that has a balcony. I sense that you love the outdoors, coming from the mountains and all. It has an amazing view and I think you will love it. Plus it's across from Patrick's office, so if your doors are open, you can see each other. We can start there. Oh, and I have a few dealerships set up with some vehicle choices. I imaging you a being a truck guy, but around here, that may not be economical. I also don't see you in a hybrid, so I have some SUV's with a possible truck combo set up. Sorry for getting excited, but this is fun for me," she says smiling.

When the day is done, I have a sweet office set up and a brand new badass jeep sitting in the driveway. Mary cooked an incredible pasta dinner. She said that she knows that carbs are the devil but feels that I need it with the day we had.

I'm not used to having a full table set with flowers and place settings. I feel a little off. Until Patrick walks in and sits down. His smile lights up the room.

"Grab your plate," he says grabbing his and standing.

"What are you doing?" I ask as I grab mine and stand.

"This isn't you and this isn't me. This table is for parties and family, this is not us," he says walking out and I follow.

He sets his plate down on the little table set off to the side of the kitchen. "This is more like it."

I sit down and smile. "Yeah, this is more like it."

We eat and he tells me about his day and I imagine this as being a regular occurrence.

"There will be rooms in this house we may never use. I know this. I want it to be home, though. Anytime you feel like it's not, you need to tell me," he says.

"It is a lot, but Patrick. I love it. It can be overwhelming, but I'm so grateful to call this ours. I will treasure each and every inch of the space and will always make sure it feels like home to us both."

"I love that about you. It is home," he says.

"Our home," I say.

We finish our dinner and Patrick grabs my hand and pulls me downstairs to what I discovered earlier was a full theater room.

There's a popcorn machine, soda fountain, and kegerator. We make popcorn and pour ourselves beers and sit down in two recliners as Patrick dims the lights and starts a movie.

I start laughing immediately. "As you wish," I say as the opening credits roll.

Chapter Twenty-Nine

Patrick

William starts his new job today. I get up extra early and make us breakfast and coffee. I also pack him a lunch. We walk hand and hand to our vehicles and give each other a kiss goodbye as we part ways.

It's a routine that I want to make an everyday thing. We exchange a few texts throughout the day. He's having a good day, which makes me so happy. It would suck if his first day went bad.

I run out for lunch and as I grab a salad, I see babies everywhere. I've got the bug and I got it bad. I need to stop thinking about it. I'm in a new relationship, and can't go all wanting babies already. It's an obstacle I don't think we are ready for anyways.

I get home before William. Mary has dinner staying warm in the oven as she leaves for the day. I run up and change into some basketball shorts and head to the exercise room. I really love this house, but it's so damn big.

I get some cardio in and I'm a sweaty mess when I hear William shouting for me.

"In here babe!" I yell out pushing out one more set of pull ups.

"Fuck, you are sexy all sweaty and shit," he says as he comes in and leans against the doorframe.

"I like it when it's you that makes me that way," I smile as I drop to the floor and wipe my face off with a towel.

He tosses me a bottle of water and I chug half of it down.

"I also like to watch your throat when you swallow," his voice lowers as he adjusts himself.

I walk over and lower myself to my knees. Before I'm all the way to the floor, he has his belt and pants undone. He lifts my face with one finger under my chin.

I look up and see his lips slightly parted, "Suck me, Patrick."

I pull his pants down his hips so that just part of his hard cock is exposed and pressed against his stomach.

I flatten my tongue against it and run it hard up to the tip. I see a small drop of precum and I lick it up.

"I said, suck, not lick, Patrick," he growls and I gasp loving his dominant side.

I push his pants to the floor and place my hands on his hips, "Remember that one time when I held you against me?" I say looking up through my lashes and opening my mouth.

"I do," he says growling. "Is that what you want?"

I nod my head as he taps his cock against my tongue and I relax my throat, knowing what's coming.

He slides in slowly as I close my lips around him. Breathing slowing through my nose, I feel his cock touch the back of my throat. I swallow as he growls.

Placing his hands on either side of my face, he pulls me against him as he slides further down. I dig my hands into his hips and close my eyes as they start to tear up.

He pulls me off with a pop and lets me catch my breath as he pushes his cock back in my mouth until I'm pressed back up against him again. I love how this feels and understand why he enjoyed it so much.

I reach down and grab his balls, slipping a finger into his ass. He fucks my mouth a little faster only giving me a short amount of time to take in a breath. I try to breathe through my nose as much as I can.

I feel his balls and ass tighten and know he's almost there. My face is flat against his stomach, his cock is down my throat and when I swallow, he blows. The guttural moan has my balls tingling.

He releases my head and falls to his knees. I wipe my mouth just before he takes my lips with his. He reaches down into my shorts wrapping his hand around my cock. He continues to kiss me as he strokes, and I gasp as I come into his hand.

"That was a hell of a welcome home from my first day at work," he says laughing.

"I think it needs to be another routine," I say kissing him.

"What do you mean?" he says holding my face and looking into my eyes.

"I mean. I loved how we started our day and I want that to be how we start each day. I know that we won't always end it with sex, but damn I really enjoyed that and would love for us to have something like this on the daily. I mean we are two very sexual men. I know we will have our off days, but I would love for us to have something like this to look forward to at the end of each day," I say tilting my head.

"I would certainly love to try. It may be unrealistic to do every day, but I'm game to put in the effort," he says kissing me again.

"Did I tell you today that I love you?" I smile.

"You did, but that's something I will never accept as being a constant. No matter what, we tell each other each and every day. Multiple times, if possible, of our love to each other," he says standing and pulling me to my feet.

"That's a deal I am more than willing to promise to," I say pulling him in and hugging him.

"I love you too, Patrick."

Chapter-Thirty

Buddy

I feel like I'm living in a dream. The house is huge. We have a home theater room, an exercise room, an infinity pool, and a maid. It's definitely not what I'm used to. I want it to be normal, I don't want to be caught up in the wealth that I feel like I've been dumped into. That's not me. I will always appreciate it. I see the empty rooms and think about how I can fill them. How can I share this wonderful home?

"Patrick? Can I ask you something?" I say as we lay in bed.

"Of course, anything," he responds.

"This house is so big. It feels like home, don't get me wrong, but I keep wondering if there is something we can do to make it more," I say.

"What do you have in mind?" he asks.

"We are just starting out, I know and I love how we can be open and free here, but what do you think about maybe applying for foster care?" I say.

"Human or pet?" he says making a weird face.

"Either, really. Oh my God, I would love to get a dog or a cat or both. I didn't even think of that," I say starting to get excited.

I see his face fall.

"Patrick? Babe? Why did your face just fall?" I ask.

"I would love to get a pet or two. I just have been really struggling lately but I didn't want to say anything. We are so new and I don't think we are ready," he says.

"Who is ever ready? Babe, I want our home to be filled with laughter and love. Maybe start out with a few pets and go to humans? We may want to look into it now. I can't imagine that foster care or even adoption is easy for our lifestyle. What do you think? Do you want to start looking into it? It could be a year or longer before anything even happens. Until then, I would love to go and rescue some fur babies," I say smiling.

"Yes. Yes on both. I would love that," he says coming over and pulling me into a hug.

We agree to meet at the local shelter after work the next day. I guess I should figure out if I can take care of an animal before I take on the human species.

I want to take them all home. "This may have not been a good idea."

"Only one, Patrick," I say rubbing his back and laughing.

"But they all look so sad," he says walking from pen to pen.

"You can't take just one," the handler says smiling.

"Yeah, that's a good pitch, but we only want one," I say trying to stay strong.

"Okay, well, I have something unconventional. If you would just give me the chance to show you," she says.

We follow her down the aisle of cages and I have to pull Patrick away from each one. It's not easy for me either, there are some really sweet looking animals in here.

We get to the end and see a dog cuddled up with a smaller cat.

"Oh fuck me now," I say pressing my face against the glass.

"That's Dixie. She's a pit mix and was brought in with that little tabby mix that we call Princess. They cannot be separated. We tried and they both go nuts. No one will take them both, but we refuse to separate them," she says opening the door.

Patrick walks right in and sits down. Dixie gingerly walks over and sits directly in front of him. Princess yawns and stretches and then walks over and starts rubbing against his leg. The attendant and I just stand and stare as she crawls up into his lap. He pets her and scratches Dixie who tries to crawl into his lap as well. Patrick laughs and lays down on the floor. Both the dog and the cat push themselves closer.

"Oh, well, I don't want to assume anything, but I think your boyfriend has established himself as a friend," she says smiling.

I want to know how they will react to me. It's not just about him here. I walk over and sit with my legs crossed in front of Patrick. I'm surprised when Princess walks over and smells me up and down, eventually laying between the two of us. Dixie does the same and the two of them snuggle together between me and Patrick.

Touching us both, they fall asleep. “Yeah, I think we are done here. These two are coming home with us.”

I laugh when we go to the pet store to get all the supplies we need for these two. Princess sits on Dixie’s back the whole time. People take pictures. I keep thinking viral internet with these two. They are definitely unique. What is even more special? When we get them home and they somehow find our bedroom. Patrick and I find ourselves on the edge of the bed with these two between us. This is definitely something we needed.

Chapter Thirty-One

Patrick

One Year Later

Two babies were born. We have a pseudo niece and nephew. Holding the babies make me really want one of my own. Marissa and Mick have a little boy and Presley Ann and Logan have a little girl. They were born a mere few weeks apart.

We have Princess and Dixie and those two have been an amazing duo. But to have a baby is what I really want. It just doesn't seem to be in the cards.

We signed up foster care and have been emergency ones more times than I can count. Nothing long term and it tore our hearts out each and every time.

It's the holidays and we decide to bring everyone who can come out to LA. Logan allows for the jet to be used and we have all the rooms set up and ready to go.

Mary helps to set up a pretty amazing feast. We see the headlights come up the driveway and steady ourselves. We are both so excited to see everyone.

The door opens and everyone runs in. I'm overwhelmed by all the hugs.

Mary was wonderful with making sure there were highchairs there for the little ones. The babies were amazing and I feel that stupid pull to my chest.

The dinner was nothing less than perfect. I have my family here. What more do I need?

There are babies on the floor playing with Dixie and Princess. They are barely sitting up, but they have these little foam chairs that keep them upright and it's adorable. My friends and family are here, and I have the man of my dreams in my arms.

My phone rings and I look at it and immediately to William. "Umm, babe."

"What's wrong?" he asks standing.

"There was a baby dropped off at the local fire department and they want to know if we can take him in," I say smiling as my heart beats out of my chest.

"Fuck yes. Oh, no, I mean. Of course, we can," he says standing up and starting to pace.

With our family and friends at our backs, we open the door to a social worker holding a baby carrier with wide eyes. She runs down the details, hand us some paperwork, some baby supplies, and leaves us with a sleeping baby.

"What the fuck do we do now?" I say looking at this little sleeping angel.

Presley Ann steps up and says, "You find a place for this little sweetheart to sleep. He's going to wake up soon and we need to be ready."

Between her and Marissa, we have plenty of bottles prepared and ready. They decide to share a baby pen between them and give us the extra one. I'm going crazy but everyone else seems calm.

This is the first time we've gotten a baby. Usually, it's older kids. Those talk and can tell you what they want and shit. This is a fresh newborn.

His name is Damon and he is amazingly calm. We don't know the whole situation, but with only a slight whine, a bottle calms him. A cry results in a diaper change and he's smiling. I can't believe how attached I get to him in such a short time.

He's perfect.

Until about two o'clock in the morning, when all hell breaks loose. We have the playpen in our room and the scream that comes from this little tiny baby is huge. I don't understand what is happening. I'm woken from a dead ass sleep.

"Doc, shut off the alarm!" I yell.

"It's the baby," he yells back and rolls out of bed, running for the playpen and reaching in for Damon.

"How is that coming out of that little body?" I groan.

All of a sudden, I hear the song of the babies. Cries can be heard throughout the whole entire house. This is a big house. Yet, the cries are incredibly loud.

"Oh, shit," William says bouncing up and down and rubbing Damon's back.

I pull back his diaper and see that he needs to be changed. He literally has shit all over his back. I grab a onesie and a diaper and William follows me into the bathroom.

This little dude is wailing and throwing his arms and legs everywhere. We get him stripped down and washed off. A new diaper and onesie on, he seems to calm a little.

We walk down to the kitchen and we are greeted by baby central. The crying slowly starts to die down. Bottles are warmed and babies are sucking them down until there is finally silence. Everyone is awake in the house. I dim the lights and we all take seats around the huge sectional. I look around and smile. The guys are almost completely asleep, the moms are whispering to each other. William and I are snuggled together looking at this little baby. He looks up at me and smiles.

"That was intense," he whispers. "He is so beautiful, though."

"He really is," I say. "I don't want to get too close though. You know how this usually goes."

"He was abandoned at a fire station, though. I think this one is going to be different. At least, I'm hoping," he says leaning over and giving me a kiss.

"I just fear getting too attached," I say.

One by one, the rest of the group gets up and returns to their rooms leaving us alone.

"I don't want to put him down but I know that's not healthy. I just don't want a mini apocalypse to break out again," he says chuckling.

We look down as Damon puckers his lips and stretches out his arms. My heart pings again.

"I'm lost in this, Doc. I really want to keep him. How can this be in one night? After all the commotion he caused tonight, I welcome it. I want it," I say kissing his head.

"I get it. I feel it too. I'm not much of a praying man, but I'm asking God to grant us this," he says.

The next day the social worker shows up to check in on things. She looks around at all the babies in the room and smiles.

"I guess with the holidays, you have family here. This is good. I hope everything was okay last night?" she asks.

"We had a little bit of a breakdown and all the babies were going off at the same time, but we handled it. Does he have a story? Anything you can tell us?" I ask.

"There were a few pictures with him and a note. I don't think the mother will come back. The note was pretty clear that she couldn't care for him and wanted only the best. I know you are signed up for emergency care, but I also know that you have filed for long term as well. Any chance you would be up for adoption? Not saying it will automatically go that way, but I want to make clear your intentions and stand by you if that is your goal," she questions.

"Yes," we both say in unison.

"Perfect. I'll get the documents ready and we will go from there," she stands and looks around the room. "Knowing you have a great support system will work in your favor. Even though your relationship is not considered conventional, yet in this state, it's not a deal breaker. I think you will be fine. Stay strong, boys. I'll be in contact," she says as she leaves.

"Well, I guess we may need to get a room ready for this little one. Permanent or not, I think he deserves it," William says rocking a sleeping Damon in his arms.

Chapter Thirty-Two

Buddy

The next day it's like the dads and moms are on a mission. Patrick and the girls all leave us with the babies as they head out to get what we need for Damon.

The dads all spend the day changing diapers, soothe whining babies and I feel closer to them than ever.

"Who would have thought that our first holiday together we would be dealing with all this," I say laughing.

Logan smiles as he bounces Lilly on his lap. "My life is complete. I found love and I produced this incredible little human in the process. I'm overwhelmed and sleep deprived, but never happier," he says as Lilly squeals slapping his face.

I'm left with the newborn. There is no interaction between us, but I'm still connecting with this little human. His little lips press together and he blows bubbles.

I wipe them away and set him on my shoulder. I really pray that he stays. I want him to be here. I need this little human to stay. I need him.

I love that everyone is so enthusiastic to set up a room for Damon. All the guys get together and put together the crib and changing table. When it's finished, I look around and smile.

"You are all wonderful. Thank you. Let's just pray that we get to keep him," I say walking out and head outside.

Mick follows and as soon as I tuck my head by the railing overlooking LA, I feel his arm wrap around me.

"Nothing is a guarantee in this fucking life. But that little man up there needs you. Even if it's temporary. I'm so proud of you, man. You've come so far and I pray that everything works out. If it doesn't, it will still be okay. You will get the family you deserve. Or you will be left with just us. I think we are all pretty amazing, but I know it's not everything you want. Have faith. I do," he says pulling me into a hug.

"Thank you. I appreciate that. I'm praying for that too. I love this little dude, so much. I can't imagine him not being here. This is where he belongs. I feel this in my heart," I say looking up at the light that is coming from what now is his bedroom.

We head back in and Patrick comes walking down the steps. He pulls me in and whispers in my ear, "You okay, Doc?"

"I will be. No matter what. I got you and all these loony people in my life," I look over at Mick who is bouncing Junior on his lap and singing some weird song that I'm sure he just made up.

The only thing missing is my mom. She started dating someone and decided not to come with everyone else but will be coming right after Christmas and staying for New Year's. We had promised to go there, but with the crew coming here, she was fine with coming out instead.

The group here will be heading back Christmas Eve. They want to be home with their babies for the actual holiday. I can certainly understand that. They need to start their own traditions with their families.

"Damon loves the crib. Little man is out," Patrick says holding a new baby monitor.

It is camera equipped, so I can see him lying in the crib with his mouth hanging open and a little drool running down.

I chuckle and say, "Damn, he's already starting to take on your characteristics."

"Funny. Real funny. I'm okay with that though. You drool, little man," Patrick says smiling.

We have one last dinner together before the crew leaves tomorrow. There is laughter around the table. Babies laughing and babies crying. I hold Patrick's hand and clear my throat.

"Thank you all for coming. I hope we make this a tradition for years to come. Maybe switch where we go each time, but try to make sure we spend it all together. Thank you for being such a great support system with Damon. I'm a little scared to not have you all around," I say.

"You got this dad," Mick says lifting his beer.

I love hearing that word. Dad. I just hope it sticks.

We have another mini apocalypse right around the same time again that night. The amount of shit this little body produces is kind of scary.

Patrick's face is priceless. I can tell he's not breathing through his nose and the faces he is making are hilarious.

"Oh. God. Oh. Dude. How do you manage to get this all the way up your back? Do we need to go up a size or what?" he says gagging.

"Maybe it's too loose? Hell if I know," I say laughing. "Your face, though."

"Don't you smell it? It's like toxic waste. Even my shit doesn't stink this bad," he says wrapping up the dirty diaper and dropping it in the diaper pail.

∞ ∞ ∞

It's like a revolving door. As soon as the crew leaves, my mom and her new boyfriend arrive. His name is Kip.

I was really surprised when she said he was coming with her. I was nervous about how he was going to react and treat us. I was very much prepared to punch him or have to kick him out of our house.

I was more surprised when he didn't bat an eye when he walked into the house. He shook both my hand and Patrick's. He asked for a beer and relaxed on the couch making himself at home.

When we introduced Damon to them, he tucked him into his arms and made baby noises and laughed when Damon responded with smiles.

I stood and watched in awe. "Where the hell did you meet him and how the hell did you get so lucky?"

"I met him on Facebook, actually. He wanted to join our reading group and I thought it was weird for a man to want to join, but he did and it just went from there. He's really sweet," my mom says.

"Well, he seems cool with me and Patrick. I'm a little surprised, to be honest," I say handing her a glass of wine.

"I told him on our first date. I wanted it out there and I wanted to see his reaction. He shrugged and said that men have been gay for centuries. It's about time they can live out in the open and be honest. I knew then he was a keeper," she says holding up her wine glass and taking a sip.

"I'm happy for you, momma. 'Bout time you found someone worth your time," I say taking a swig of my beer.

Chapter Thirty-Three

Patrick

The social worker shows up on Christmas Eve. I'm surprised that she's here.

"Our work is never done. I wanted to just touch base and give you some news," she says.

"Oh, man. That doesn't sound good," I say pulling William in close to prepare for the news.

"Well, it's not bad, just some obstacles. It seems there are two families that have come forward to also request to adopt. The issue of you two being gay is not a problem. However, the fact that the two of you are not married seems to be," she says. "It doesn't mean you won't be in the running for the adoption, but it could be used against you."

"Well, then let's get you two married," I hear coming from William's mom. "Kip is ordained and can do it anytime."

"A Christmas wedding. Always wanted to do one of those," Kip says walking over and putting his arm around ma.

"It's Christmas Eve. Nothing is open for us to even file for a license," William says.

"I have some contacts. Let me see what I can do. I'll be in touch before the end of the day. We may have you two married before the night is through," the social worker says as she gets ready to leave. "I told you that I was in your corner. I see how badly you want Damon. I want that for him too."

She leaves and William immediately starts pacing. "This is not how this was supposed to happen. This isn't right."

He walks to the door and grabs his keys and walks out. I'm left standing between Kip and his mom worried that he's going to leave me.

"What just happened?" I say bending down and placing my hands on my knees.

I try calling his phone, but he doesn't pick up. It seems like hours until he finally walks back into the door. He's holding a bouquet of flowers. I stand from the couch and walk over to him.

He bends to one knee and reaches out for my hand. "I love you. I love what we are starting here. Nothing has been conventional in our relationship. My coming out, Damon coming into our lives or what I'm about to do. I want you to be a part of my life, forever. I wanted to do something grand when I proposed. It seems like life won't let us do anything conventionally. I'm prepared to have this continue to happen. It's okay because now I know to expect the unexpected. Life is out of our control. However, my life couldn't be more perfect. You know how I love to have control but knowing that the best things seem to happen when it's not in control is now what I appreciate most. Patrick. Will you be my husband, my life, my love and my constant?"

The room disappears and I only see him. Kneeling before me and professing his love.

"This is perfect. This is us. I couldn't even imagine a more perfect proposal. I would love to be your husband," I say leaning down and pressing my lips to his.

We get our license a few hours later and, on the patio, overlooking the city, we exchange our vows with Kip officiating.

No, it wasn't what we had expected, but I feel like it was even better. His mom cried when we kissed. She played photographer and caught some amazing pictures. My favorite was us in an embrace as the sun set over the valley. We send it to our friends and get bombarded with responses.

I post it and change my status to married. Patrick Daniel Ross and William Lee Hanson are now joined in holy matrimony.

I decide to take on his name with a hyphen. It's weird knowing his mom is in the house, but she tells us to go spend some time together. She has Damon and between her and Kip, that little man is going to be spoiled.

We enter the bedroom and William closes the door. "I can't believe we are married. Merry Christmas, husband."

"Merry Christmas," I say as I drop to my knees and show him how much I love him.

We end up consummating the marriage with my legs wrapped around him and him deep inside me. I see stars as I come on my stomach as he grunts out his release. We don't even clean up after. We roll into each other and quickly fall asleep in each other's arms. A perfect ending.

Epilogue

Patrick

It took almost a year of constant court hearings and fighting until we were finally able to adopt Damon. Our friends come out to celebrate with us.

Damon Alan Ross-Hanson. It's a mouth full.

We've had our challenges. Sleepless nights and constant poop patrol. This kid can shit with the best of them. But to see him smile is nothing short of bliss.

He could swim before he could walk. We wanted to make sure the pool would be safe with him. He said "Dada" to William first. I was okay with that because he turned to me and said it again shortly after.

I don't know what will be in store for us as he gets older. Will he get teased by having two dads? Will he get bullied about being gay even if he isn't because his dads are? We attended classes with other gay parents. We continue to learn a lot.

No matter what comes our way, we vow to make sure he knows he is loved.

He's the most important thing after all.

Logan comes over and pulls me into a hug. "Happy for you, brother."

"You are the reason for all of this, you know? Marissa and Mick. William and me. It all started when you wanted to get away for a sabbatical. This was the result of your impulse," I say looking up at him.

"Perfect, right? You're welcome," he says smiling.

"It is perfect. Who knew letting go of control would bring everything I've always wanted?" I say.

I laugh as I watch Damon shove icing from his cupcake into his mouth. William walks over and wraps his arms around me.

"I love you. It was a bumpy start but I can't say how anything could be more perfect than it is now. You, Damon and me are family and I can't imagine life without you both," he says kissing my neck.

"It's perfect. I love you so much. Thank you for sticking by me and my crazy," I say leaning into him.

Moments like this need to be treasured. A gay man with an awesome husband and a perfect son that I wouldn't have had if it weren't for my boss going off the deep end.

"Logan," I say needing to voice this even though I had told him a few minutes ago.

He comes to stand next to me and I get everyone's attention.

"This. Us. All started with this man thinking he needed a break. Look what the hell he did," I laugh.

Everyone else joins in laughing. "Anyways. Thank you. My boss, my best friend, my brother. You are at fault and I'm so happy that you are. Look at this. Look at what you did."

"Well, unless you are seeing something different, I think it's pretty amazing what I did. Look at us," Logan says.

Everyone gathers in a circle and embraces with laughter. A family from different coasts. A family of different incomes and stature. A family with different sexual preferences.

It all doesn't matter. We are a family. Built out of love.

Acknowledgements

I was so excited to tell Patrick's story. I hope you all enjoyed it as much as I did writing it.

Thank you to my Alpha readers, Stephanie M. and Pam. I love your passion for my stories and all your help in the process.

Beta Babes! Thank you for being there for me. Your feedback is always appreciated.

Jackie, thank you again for being my last set of eyes. I know it drives you crazy having to wait.

Melissa Deanching, thank you for your inspiring photo of Cody Smith and thanks to Reggie for always working with me.

Cody Smith, my amazing friend. You are my Patrick. Your antics and smile always seem to brighten my day. Thank you for your vibrant presence on this earth. I'm so grateful to have met you and have you grace my cover.

To the readers, thank you for giving me a reason to continue on this crazy journey as an author.

This series may have come to an end, but guess what? Rev will be coming to you in a new spinoff series in The Lion's Den MC. Three books (so far planned) with Rev'd, KO'd and Chop'd. This one is going to push my limits from being the light hearted story teller to a more grittier style of writing. Stay tuned!

About the Author

CJ Allison is a divorced mother of a grown son. She has two crazy cats and spends her days in a high walled cubicle behind duel monitors managing projects and a staff of eleven.

In her spare time, she writes. The characters tap dance in her head until she gets them down on paper. It's a crazy life.

Make sure you follow her on social media!

Amazon Author Page: https://www.amazon.com/C-J-Allison/e/B071WKGCFZ/ref=ntt_dp_epwbk_0
Author Website: https://cjallisonauthor.wixsite.com/mysite
Author Facebook Fan Page: https://www.facebook.com/cjallisonauthor/
Goodreads: https://www.goodreads.com/author/show/16905737.C_J_Allison
Instagram: https://www.instagram.com/c.j.allisonauthor/
Twitter: @cjallisonauthor
Bookbub: @cjallisonauthor
Reader Group: https://www.facebook.com/groups/212148038121240 9/

Made in the USA
Middletown, DE
27 September 2021

48300869R00129